SINS OF THE SON

FRANK LUCIANUS

Nothing personal, it's just business.

— Otto Berman

CONTENTS

"IN NOMINE PATRIS"

Giuliani Family

The crimson Fiat Spider was slowly driving down Oak Street close to 10 a.m. The sound of crunching leaves beneath its tires and the gentle hum of its engine were the neighborhood's only disturbances. It was late autumn and the car's occupants were heading to the Baldinotti Mansion, Oak Street, Number 18. Behind its tinted windows was a man in a white suit loading bullets in his Thompson 1928.

The car pulled up in front of the mansion and there were two guards standing outside its wrought iron gates. When the guards reached for their guns inside their, it was too late. One of the Fiat rear windows lowered, the barrel of the Thompson peeking out. Two loud, instantaneous bangs sounded off the gates and both guards fell. Life was ending so abruptly for them. The backseat door of the Fiat opened and a man in a white suit stepped out, reloading. The barrel of his gun was still smoking as he walked slowly towards the guards' bodies, careful to not get his polished white shoes dirty. The man crouched. *"In Nomine Patris et Fili et spiritus Sancti. Amen,"* the man said signing the cross over his chest, and put two more bullets between their eyes. A faint smile curved/crept up his face as he adjusted his hat and stepped over the bodies. He pushed open the double iron doors which let out a long, painful screech. The man looked upwards, his jaw sticking out from the white hat. He saw a fat man, standing behind the glass on the second floor, closing the curtains.

The man in the white suit gingerly walked through the withered garden. The grass smell reminded him of the days he used to visit this place and play when he was little boy. His father was once an ally of the Baldinotti's but nowadays, Davide was paying tributes for protection. Those days were now a distant memory. The trees in the courtyard had no leaves and the fountain was covered in moss. The garden had been neglected, just like the fat man on the second floor, awaiting his demise. The man in the white suit stood, for a moment, praying outside the double wooden doors, engraved with the huge letter, 'B'. Taking a deep breath, he pushed them open, and crossed the carpet to the marble staircase. His footsteps echoed through the empty hallway as he ascended to the second floor. He walked carefully but with determination. The wealth of fat man would go to waste in moments. Not long from now, his mansion would be in ruins; a destroyed garden permeated by death. The man looked down the corridor seeing a guard stationed outside another engraved door. A second series of gunshots sounded, and the guard dropped to the ground, bleeding. His pained, final breaths echoed through the hallway of the empty mansion . The man in the white suit stepped over him and opened the wooden door, heading to the Davide's office.

He was sitting behind his mahogany desk, piled high with money. It was a shame he wouldn't see it again, after today. Davide who was dressed in a red silk robe, reached for his gun under the desk, but the click of the loaded Thompson stopped him cold. The gun was pointed at him. The man in the white suit casually took off his hat and hung it on the coat rack, revealing his dark hair and clean-shaved face.

"I wouldn't do that if I were you, Davide." the man said.

"Wh…what do you want? What is the meaning of this?" Davide said with a heavy Italian accent, spitting as he talked. His face beaded with sweat and he tried wiping it off with his sleeve, to no avail.

"Oh, you know full well what I want. You broke the rules, didn't you?"

"I don't know what you're talking about, Francesco. I paid my share this month, no?"

"This isn't about the commission. Let's cut the crap." Francesco said.

"Tell Don Luca—tell him I've been loyal to Familia Giuliani since we came from Sicily. You forget so easily?"

"You are the one who forgets. You are the one who forgets who's been protecting you all this time. *Who* is protecting you?"

"Familia Giuliani, ovviamente!"

"Then why were you dining with Michael Lombardi three nights ago?"

With an imposing look on his face, Francesco closed their distance and took a seat across from Davide, his gun still pointed at the fat man's neck. He was pale as paper; his eyes stretching on the mention of the name Lombardi.

"I—you know, I work as a watcher. I want to infiltrate Familia Lombardi, help you with their secrets, you understand, right?"

"Sabina Baldinotti, 72 Port Street New York, Fourth Floor."

"No!"

"Yes, Davide."

"You wouldn't bring my Bambina into this."

Francesco raised the Thompson, pointing at the fat man's head.

"You will not leave this room and you know that. Try doing something good for your family, for once"

"You are a monster, Francesco! Where is your honor?"

"Where is the honor in betraying our family Davide? What did they offer you? Money? Guns?"

Davide tried wiping the sweat from his face once again. His chest was aching, and he knew he had no other option.

"They offered me nothing. I wanted safe passage for my *Bambina*. They only are planning to take charge of New York Harbor. You failed Giuliani. Lombardi surpassed you."

Francesco responded only with a long halfhearted laugh. He found the fat man funny. All these years, Davide was nothing but a snake; a burden the Giuliani family was carrying. His businesses were failing, and his wife had abandoned him. Even his guards weren't ready to die for him.

"So, it was all for protection. Do you feel safe now Davide? I'll make sure to let your daughter know that you cared for her."

"Empty threats, Francesco. You can kill me now but know the Giulianis are finished. Remember that."

"In Nomine Patris et Fili et Spiritus Sancti. Amen"

"You still do that shit, Francesco?"

"It's what keeps me human. Forgiveness by God. I wouldn't expect you to understand."

"You are a pompous bast…"

A loud shot filled the room. Davide fell backward off his chair, his last sentence left unfinished. His large body was lying on the wooden floor, soaked in blood, his brains splattered on the wall behind.. "In Nomine Patris" he scoffed. "Fuck, you don't deserve that kind of respect."

Francesco got up and headed towards the exit. He

took his hat and delicately adjusted it on his head. As he was walking through the mansion 's yard, two police officers arrived inspecting the bodies out front. Francesco held out his arms and blessed them with a brilliant, false smile.

"Jonathan! Terry!" he shouted with pretended enthusiasm.

The two policemen took their attention off the bodies and turned towards him.

"Francesco? What is this?"

"You know how things go sometimes. We are boys. Sometimes we play and sometimes we fight!"

"It is the middle of the day. Do you expect us to let you walk?"

"Nobody's watching, right? Look, the streets are empty."

"We'll have to call it in. And the price just doubled. This a new level of shit to deal with."

"Okay Terry, relax! I'll make sure to slip something extra for you two this month. Okay?"

The two policemen agreed wanly. Terry lifted his police radio from his cop car. "Two victims, white males, 18 Oak Street. Baldinotti Mansion . Probably more bodies inside. No perpetrator at the scene." Terry exaggerated with cool. "Dispatch, sending two units over," a female voice was heard over the receiver.

Francesco smiled and patted Terry, friendlily on the cheek.

"The Giuliani family thanks you two for your services. We'll not forget you."

"You better not," Jonathan murmured as he walked inside of the Mansion .

Francesco left Terry, crouching over the dead guards, and crossed the street towards the crimson Fiat Spider. His driver, dressed in a white suit, like Francesco, was waiting outside in front of the car, reclining against the door, nursing a cigarette. Francesco climbed into the passenger seat. His smile left as quickly as it came.

"Quite a mess you made, Francesco." the driver said, seeing the blood on his boss' suit. "The job is done. Let's go." The driver took one last drag before they headed back to the Giuliani Mansion .

2

─────

A FAMILY DINNER

Giuliani Family

It was a 30-minute drive from the Baldinotti Mansion to the Giuliani Mansion Estate, outside New York City. Francesco's driver parked the Spider, noting that there were no guards at the front gate.

"Francesco, please tell your father everything," the driver said closing the driver-side door. Francesco grunted and kept walking.

The Giuliani Mansion was a fascinating place. The garden in the front had well-trimmed trees and plants in assorted shapes and sizes. There was a small marble fountain hidden behind the trees and statues arrayed in the area. The statues were inspired by the Renaissance with a few Michelangelo models. The Giuliani greats loved Michelangelo.

Francesco walked towards the main entrance, snubbing the salutes of the two guards waiting outside. He hastily entered and slammed the door behind him. One of the guards tried speaking but the door had already closed. A faint "They are having dinner" reached Francesco's ears as he headed towards the family dining room. The hazy afternoon sun poured in through the glass partition, bathing the wall in light. This combined with the sweet flickering from the fireplace, created a peaceful ambiance. His family was already eating at the grand mahogany table. The table could comfortably host ten persons, maybe more, but just three were enjoying their meal today; his beloved father, mother, and not-so-friendly little brother. They were talking quietly enjoying a dish of Baccala alla Vicentina. Francesco walked in, pulled up a chair and served himself, interrupting the conversation.

"Is it done, Francesco?" his father, Luca asked without taking his eyes from his plate.

"Yes, father. Just as we discussed," Francesco said.

"Luca, please. We have said this over and over again. No family business at the table."

"Bene Sofia. Bene. I just wanted to make sure everything was okay." Luca grunted as he filled his plate with more food. For how slim the old man was, he was eating a lot more than someone his age.

"And enough with the food, leave some for the kids. A man your age should be more careful."

"Madre, it's ok. Let the man eat. At his age, it will be the last thing he'll do," Francesco's brother said chuckling.

His mother gave him a menacing look; a look everyone in the family learned to dread.

"You should be ashamed, Manuel! Talking to father like this."

"Why do you care Francesco?"

"You have a big mouth for a seventeen-year-old. Show some respect. This is our father!"

"Like you would know. You are never around Francesco!"

"And I still respect him more than you."

Manuel wanted to continue arguing with his big brother but was interrupted by Luca. "Enough! Can an old man eat in peace? Finish your dinner, we'll talk afterward Francesco." Sofia nodded, enjoying her meal.

The rest of the time went on without much talking, only the sound of forks and spoons, tinkling on the porcelain, could be heard, echoing through the dining hall. Minutes later, Manuel headed to his room while Sofia cleared the table. "Would you like a glass of wine my love?" Luca nodded please as he wiped his lips with a silk towel.

Sofia left with a huge bin of dirty dishes. Luca sat back in his chair and slowly turned towards Francesco.

"So?" he said, waiting for Francesco to start talking.

"As you said. Davide was home. Everyone was out even most of the guards."

"Most?"

"Yes, father. There were two at the front gate and one outside his office."

"They're still loyal? How impressive!"

"Yeah, but I dealt with it."

"So, how is my dear friend Davide doing?"

"He seemed a little tense. I left him looking a little more peaceful than I found him."

"Bene. Bene. So, what was this meeting with Lombardis about? What business does he have with them?"

The conversation was disrupted by Sofia. She entered the room holding a salver with three crystal glasses of wine. The middle-aged woman carefully placed one in front of Luca and then Francesco and took a seat beside her husband.

"Sofia. This is important. Why don't you go help clean the dishes?"

"I'm part of this business too, Luca. Please, you'd be lost without me, dear."

Luca smiled delightedly. He loved his wife and knew she was telling him the truth. The old man would be long gone by now if it wasn't for her perseverance. Sofia took a sip of wine and walked away but came back.

"Don't let me interrupt you, then."

"So, back to the meeting."

"Davide said something about the Lombardis wanting to take control of New York harbor." Francesco said.

"So, they plan to take the city from us?"

"That's what Davide said. But you know…"

"That fat man can't be trusted even on his deathbed."

"Sofia, please. Davide is family. Show some respect for the dead for God's sake."

Sofia paused and made the sign of the cross. Francesco chuckled as his father looked skeptical.

"I didn't expect the Lombardis to start a conflict like this. Francesco, tomorrow you will head to the harbor, and talk with Elias and see what is going on."

"What if the Lombardis already have him on their payroll?"

"Remind him of how he got to be a supervisor. Remind him what the Giulianis did so her could get that position."

Francesco smiled as the three remained in silence enjoying their glasses of Barolo. Francesco finished first and got up.

"I'm going to take a nap. Tomorrow's a big day."

Sofia and Luca nodded, diving into another conversation. Francesco headed out of the dining room and straight to his room. Once upstairs, he noticed his little brother, Manuel, on the balcony, leaning over the balustrade, staring towards the backyard. Francesco walked silently behind him. A puff of smoke billowed out from Manuel's nostrils.

"That's a nasty habit," Francesco said quietly. Manuel turned around, shocked he'd been caught in the act. An expression of disgust painted his face, as he slowly turned back, staring at the withered yard across the far side of the mansion .

"Yeah, whatever."

"You should be more careful. Smoking when Mom and Dad are awake isn't wise."

"Why do you care?"

"I'm your big brother Manuel. I do care."

"That's a new one."

Francesco considered this. He didn't know how to respond. The sound of Manuel's exasperated sigh got on Francesco's nerves. "So, you're upset about what happened earlier, I get that."

"Yes, so?"

"Do as you please, Manuel. Just don't get caught by mother. She wouldn't like that."

"I won't."

Francesco was standing behind Manuel trying to intimidate him and the younger brother wouldn't even turn around. He stood there as if Francesco did exist. Francesco scoffed and left. He didn't have time for childish nonsense. Tomorrow, he had family business to take care of.

A MEETING IN THE HARBOR

Lombardi Family

The sunlight, finding its way through the half-closed shutters, was pointing directly at her face. The woman opened her eyes and stretched out on the silk sheets. She woke up before the alarm clock, as usual, and sat up. The maids have already cleaned her room. She stretched again and sleepily headed towards her bathroom. Now, her morning routine would begin.

The young lady brushed her teeth and spent at least 20 minutes brushing her long black hair. Afterward, she put on a little makeup and quickly got dressed, wearing a turquoise skirt. She headed downstairs to the kitchen. The smell of fresh-cooked eggs and bacon filled her nostrils; she could already feel her mouthwatering. The woman was hungry. She entered the door leading to the dining room. One of the maids was there, unfolding and laying out bleached-white tablecloths.

"Good morning, Miss Jessica. The usual?" the maid said warmly. Jessica nodded taking a seat on the far-right corner of the table.

"Yes, Maria. Thank you." she yawned as she placed her head against the table. She wanted so badly to sleep but she had work to do. Today was an important day for the Lombardi family. "Oh, and please bring me coffee." she moaned with the sound of her voice being stifled by the table.

"Yes, Miss Jessica. Right away."

The maid came back carrying a salver with a plate of two fried eggs and bacon, a glass of orange juice, and a cup of coffee. She set the plate down with the cups and quickly left the room softly bowing. Jessica didn't notice because her face was still resting on the table, half asleep. She reluctantly lifted her head and started eating.

Minutes later, the door to the dining room opened and an older woman entered. "Good morning my love! How come you are awake so early?" the woman asserted as she grabbed a seat beside Jessica.

"I couldn't sleep well. *Again!*"

"We should find out about those sleep problems of yours."

"I'm used to it, Mama."

"You are working too hard these days."

"The family business isn't going to run itself."

"It's been only a few weeks since you came back. You should get some rest."

"I've rested enough back in Italy. It's time for work."

"Let your father and brother worry about that, sweetie. Too much work is not good for my little one."

"Well, I didn't get a law school degree for nothing. I have to do something with it."

Their conversation was interrupted as the maid entered the room. "Good morning, Miss Christina," she said, respectfully bowing.

"Good morning, Maria! Please bring me a cup of coffee. I'll have breakfast later."

"Yes, Donna." The maid left the room after a small bow.

"So, yes. Degree or not, you are working too much. You're not twenty anymore. Enjoy some things in your life."

"Mom, I swear, if this is another talk about me closing the door to motherhood, I will really flip out."

"Oh sweetie, I don't mean to meddle, but it's been almost five years since…you know."

"Out of all days? Today? It's 8 am, Christina! For God's sake, let me enjoy my breakfast at least first." Jessica said, bordering hysterical.

Christina was shaken by her daughter's words. She sat back as the room sank into silence. That silence broke when the maid brought back the cup of coffee.

"There you go" the maid said as the silence was

displeasingly awkward after she left. Just two women sitting in the room and no one knew what to say. Jessica got up and walked away.

"Tell Papa, I'm heading to the harbor in a bit." Jessica closed the door to the dining room behind her, without waiting for her mother's reply.

She went back to her room and after half an hour, was standing in the driveway, awaiting her driver. A black 1928 Cadillac Town Sedan pulled into the driveway. The driver, a man nearly in his sixties dressed in an expensive black suit, rolled down the windows smiling. He nodded to Jessica and she entered the passenger side.

"Where to this morning, Miss Jessica?"

"To the New York Harbor, please," she said calmly looking out the window, still thinking about the conversation with her mother.

"Of course." The driver revved the engine and backed down the drive.

It was an hour drive to New York Harbor, and it was a busy Friday morning. Jessica was not in the mood for small talk. She turned on the radio just to coat the unbearable silence. She looked outside of the window as they passed by the suburbs, seeing people heading for their regular jobs at their routine times. The driver finally cleared his throat.

"So, how is your morning going, Miss Jessica?" he expressed with genuine interest. "Normal, I'd say."

"I heard you had a fight with your mother."

"Is there anything inside our house that doesn't escape?"

"You'll have to blame Miss Maria for that."

"Well, it's none of your business."

"I heard you were really hard on your mother, Miss Jessica."

"What else have you heard, Paul? Don't tell me how to behave, you are not my father."

"I've been in this house so long, Miss Jessica, I practically reared you as well."

"*Practically.*" she scoffed. "But you didn't. If you want to keep working for us, please continue doing your job only." Jessica turned up the radio's volume making any further conversation nearly impossible. A bitter smile curved at his lips.

"Don't pout, it's not good for the skin," he softly joked but the volume was high enough for Jessica to miss his remark.

Finally, they reached New York Harbor.

"I'll be ready to return home in a couple of hours. Pick me up at 12 p.m. sharp," she said slamming the car door. Jessica walked toward the main entrance as the driver sped off avoiding the crowdedness of workers and machinery. The smell of salt and sea filled her nostrils and the sun blinded her. She shielded her eyes as she fished her sunglasses from her purse. Meanwhile, the port was bustling with commotion. Trucks were passing left and right and workers were shouting to one another.

How can these people even work here, she thought to herself, disgusted with the locale?

She walked with heart in a place filled with tough-looking workers who were ordinary men working hard to make a living. Seemingly, out of nowhere, the stunning Italiana arrived and drew the attention of everyone in the harbor. Jessica liked the attention to some extent. These men couldn't offer her something she didn't already have. She had no desire for any of the workers, or much less, being in the harbor to begin with. She was here for one singular purpose: the family business. Jessica strolled to Pier 10A, where Elias, the manager could usually be found. The buzzing of the machines gave her a headache. She was sick of this place already. The smell of the churning sea combined with the strong scent of petrol and smoke emanating from the docking ships was nearly enough to turn her stomach. When she reached Pier 10A, she spotted Elias' building. She disguised her disgust and donned a beautiful smile and an air of playfulness. Acting was one small part of the business.

She rapped at the door.

"Come in." said a gravelly voice on the other side.

Jessica entered with a bright smile, wearing her sunglasses. She'd never met Elias before. The man in his sixties was dressed in a green sweater. His tiny glasses made his already large nose seem enormous. He looked tired, then again, everyone in the harbor looked tired.

"Good morning! A lovely day isn't it?" said Jessica.

"Yes, indeed. How can I help you, young lady?"

"How are you… Elias, right?"

"How do you know my name, Miss?"

"It's Jessica and it's a pleasure to finally meet you."

"Are you with the Giulianis? Did they hire a new bookkeeper?"

"Hahaha, no, no, Elias," she chuckled, " On the contrary. I'm a Lombardi."

Elias gulped knowing he was in deep shit now.

"I'm here to discuss some family business." Jessica playfully stated taking off her sunglasses and putting them on Elias desk. Elias was shocked by this woman's intimidating look.

"H—how may I help you, then?"

"You can start by telling me this: what do the Giulianis want by paying you to work for them?"

"I don't work for the Giulianis, Miss. You've must be mistaken."

Jessica smiled. She moved behind Elias, wrapping her arms, smoothly, around his skinny neck.

"Come on, Elias. Are you not going to tell me?" Jessica breathed in Elias' ear lustfully. She could feel Elias' heart racing. But, to her surprise, he shrugged off her advances.

?Jessica scoffed, returning to her seat but wasn't going to give up that easily. The real business starts now.

"Ok Elias, I tried this the easy way, but let's cut the bullshit. I know you work for the Giulianis and their guns are moving through the harbor so easily that even the homeless can't ignore it. What are they paying you?"

"As I told you, I'm not getting paid by the Giulianis."

"Loyalty, an admirable trait for a man with such a position. Should I mention to our good policemen about this little operation of yours? One probe and your entire business goes. You'll be buried in charges and fines. And we won't help you when you come seeking our protection." Jessica smirked.

Elias was a man loyal to the Giulianis but why? What do they have against him?

"You have no family or close relatives to Giulianis, Elias. What do they have on you? Tell me and maybe we could help."

"I…" Elias stuttered. "I knew this was a bad idea all along."

"Did they blackmail you? We can take care of it."

"You can't. If I tell you, I'll lose my job and lose everything."

"What about your precious life?"

Elias stared deep into Jessica's eyes. His eyes widened. "You wouldn't!"

"We wouldn't if you were a little more cooperative

here, Mr. Elias. I'm trying to make a deal, good for everyone at the table."

"Not for the Giulianis though."

"Yeah, not for the Giulianis clearly. So, what do they have on y..." Jessica couldn't manage to finish her sentence as the door opened. A man dressed in a white suit entered. Jessica could tell his Italian suit was very expensive. The man's face was cover by his long hat. He raised his head, staring first at Elias, but quickly his attention was turned toward Jessica. He gazed at her for a few seconds which seemed like ages with the heavy silence now.

The man in the white suit stood, looking at Elias as if he was waiting for an explanation. Jessica was ready to continue negotiating but was interrupted by Elias.

"This is Jessica, representing the Lombardi family," he said quickly as Jessica took her eyes from the man in the suit and looked at Elias.

"I can introduce myself, Mr. Elias, thank you." She turned towards the man in the white suit. "I am Jessica Lombardi and you are interrupting a very important meeting here."

He raised an eyebrow at the mention of the family name, but a smirk quickly curved up his lips. Jessica didn't know who the man was and wanted to slap that cocky grin off of his face. There was a confidence in him that she hadn't seen for a very long time. He looked to be about the same age as her brother, ten years older than her. She tried on a polite smile. The man took off his hat and bowed.

"How fortunate! I am representing Mr. Elias and came here to resolve an important matter. I'm Francesco Giuliani. It's a pleasure to meet you, Jessica," the man said grabbing a seat, sitting alongside Jessica. "Now, what is this meeting about?" he said with a smile, challenging hers.

4

———

THE INVESTIGATION BEGINS

The FBI

It was almost 11 pm on a Thursday night. It was storming; one of the worst storms in the past few months. The windows were rattling from every thunderbolt and Quantico was empty. There were few agents working overtime; a skeleton crew of driven agents with no one awaiting their return home.

On the third floor of the building, there was a single light on. A man in his fifties was staring at a huge pile of files lost in thought. After all these years, there was not a single thread to pull and unravel the tight-knit ball of yarn that was this agent. Welcoming the buzz, he focused on the half-empty bottle of whiskey in front of him. Just hours ago, it was sealed tight. The agent adjusted his tie, wiped the sweat off his forehead and grabbed another file. *Another piece of useless crap,* he thought as he checked his watch. 23:25. *Another day wasted.*

The man tucked the whiskey bottle and glass into the bottom drawer of his desk. He rose to his, feet grabbing his trench coat and umbrella which were still wet from when he'd gone outside for a smoke. They'd likely be damp for days since the rain didn't look to be letting up any time soon. The files he read about fifty times were strewn about his office. He'd deal with them tomorrow. It wasn't like he was making progress anyway. The agent turned off the light and made his way to the main exit but something broke the office's silence. His telephone rang, echoing off the empty hallways. He turned, his head telling himself it could wait. It was already way past his time. And the phone kept ringing. T

he man sighed, dropping his umbrella on the desk and answered the phone.

"Thomas Miller. Who is it?"

"Sir, it's me! I'm calling you from New York."

"Do you know what time it is?"

"I do sir, but this couldn't wait."

"What is it?"

"It's Davide, sir. Davide Baldinotti was murdered."

Thomas paused at the word "murdered" and took a deep breath.

"Do we have a suspect?"

"No, sir, just the usual."

"Lombardis and Giulianis? Ok, I'll head there right away."

Thomas Miller hung up before hearing what the caller had to additionally say and sat back at his desk. He opened his drawer and filled his glass with another round of whiskey. "On course," he mumbled as he drank in one shot. He got up, took his umbrella and left Quantico, heading directly to the airport.

* * *

Agent Thomas Miller arrived in New York on the forenoon of Friday , one day following Davide Baldinotti's death. The gruff-looking agent took a taxi to the Baldinotti Mansion during the sun's zenith. Thomas took a handkerchief from his pocket and swiped the sweat from his forehead. The heat was unbearable inside the taxi. The AC wasn't working, and the ride was taking way too long. Thomas kept tapping his leg nervously and his mouth was dry from dehydration. Maybe he was excited to finally catch a break on some real police work.

The taxi stopped outside the Baldinotti mansion . The man paid and got out, only to witness the yellow ribbons surrounding the house and two armed police officers at the entrance. Apart from that, it seemed like there was nothing else in the scene.

"Good morning boys. Thomas Miller with the FBI." Agent Miller took out his badge from his trench coat.

"What happened here?"

"Davide Baldinotti was executed yesterday midday."

"Any guards?"

"Three, two killed here and one inside."

"May I take a look?"

The officer didn't answer; just extended his arm towards the steps, while moving out of Agent Miller's way. aside. Thomas reached for his cigarette pack inside his trench coat finding they were soaked. He pushed a little with his finger until he found one that was dry and lit it. Slowly, he crossed the courtyard of the Baldinotti Mansion sensing the smell of the fresh-cut grass. It was an annoying smell to the veteran agent. Thomas made a few rounds in the yard looking at the ground; inspecting every detail - the trees, lawn, soil, and crevices. Crouching, he found something of interest; a foot-step on the fresh dirt. He turned towards the officers and detectives on the scene.

"I have something over here. Bring a flag here and take a picture for me."

"The forensics guys left hours ago," a detective yelled.

"Fuck," he murmured, dropping his wet cigarette next to the footprint. He stood up, wiping his hands and headed towards the mansion . The place was empty and Thomas Miller thought the rest of the Baldinottis would likely sell it once the investigation was over. It wasn't often that the rich families stuck around in the houses where their loved ones died; too many memories and too much pain haunted them. The door had bullet holes and the casings were removed and taken in as evidence back at headquarters. Thomas pushed the door gently and saw a fallen chair in an area, where the brain traces of Davide was splattered across the floor. This is was a premeditated murder. Thomas didn't even try to pull out his weapon but was afraid. This has the fingerprints of one of the big families. The Baldinottis were respected in New York City. If Davide was afraid to pull his gun, it must have been one of the other two syndicates.

Thomas crouched above the pool of blood and the smell of decay was masked, thankfully, by his cigarette's smoke. He took a long drag. Was this execution done by an automatic weapon? There were clues everywhere but nothing solid enough to stick. It reminded him of a normal crime scene where the murderer intends to leave clues but for a reason. Why did they kill Davide? Did he try to undercut someone?

Thomas picked up the phone in Davide's office and dialed.

"New York's Police Department, 5th Precinct, how may I help you."

"Thomas Miller, FBI. Badge Number 7238. Put me through to Agent Garcia."

"Certainly, Agent Miller."

A few seconds passed.

"Hello?"

"Garcia, it's me. I'm at the Baldinotti mansion."

"You've arrived already, sir? Did you find anything?"

"It seems like the idiots wrapped things up over here. Not much left to bag up."

"They took the bodies, sir, and brought them here at the morgue yesterday afternoon."

"I don't care about that. I want to talk to the police officers who were first on the scene."

"Give me a moment, sir." Some shuffling around could be heard on the other end of the line. "They are Jonathan Howards and Terry Wood, sir. They were patrolling the neighborhood around that time and called it in."

"I wanted a copy of that damn police report on my desk yesterday. Where the hell is my office anyway? Do I even have one yet?"

"Yes sir, you do. I made sure they gave you one this time."

"Good. I want you to come down here and catalog everything. There's a fresh footprint as well."

"Ok, sir. Should I tell Howards and Wood to prepare to be debriefed?"

"No. Let them be for now. I want to catch them off-guard. And please, don't make any inquiries about their report yet."

"As you wish, sir. I'm on it."

Thomas hung up sighing as he put out his glowing cigarette butt in Davide's ashtray. He left the scene having no solid leads; only a foot-print and two officers who *probably* know nothing. Nevertheless, he was ready to get to the bottom of this.

5

———

CASTELLO DI VINO

Giuliani and Lombardi Family

Francesco made sure he was close enough to see this girl who calls herself a Lombardi and Elias' desk separated the two. He took off his hat and dropped it on Elias' desk. He couldn't stop looking at the daughter of Michael Lombardi wondering why he didn't know he'd had a daughter. Francesco knew the older Lombardi offspring, Giovanni, but had never seen this girl around town, let alone heard of her. If a girl this pretty was messing with his business behind his back, Francesco would have noticed, but it seems as if he had just become aware. *This girl was definitely raised in Italy,* he thought. *She's bold and beautiful, but here in New York, she's only an exotic piece of Italian ass.* His mind was overtaken by all these thoughts as he stared at her. A stubborn silence filled the room for a long time until Jessica piped up.

"So, Mister..." she said trying to remember his name, "Francesco, right?"

"That's right," Francesco nodded.

"Are you Mr. Elias' lawyer?" she asked with a pompous smile.

Francesco laughed in surprise, a sound like gusts of wind roaring from his lungs,. "No, no. Nothing like that, my dear. I'm more of a *counselor*."

Jessica couldn't believe this man's ego. He looks like a petty gangster who thinks he's above everyone else.

"Counselor, you say? "she said. "Let's say... life counselor." he chuckled. " I advise him on decisions that would make his life better" Francesco said smirking. Jessica considered this, somehow finding him frustratingly endearing even though he was clearly a conman.

"Well then, I don't think you should be present during our business dealing, Mr. Francesco. It's not good business."

Elias had a frightened look as he turned to Francesco who didn't return his gaze. His eyes were pinned on the Lombardi girl. *This tough young woman is fascinating.* "Well, I think I'm where I'm supposed to be. Don't you agree, Elias?"

"Yes of course." the old man stuttered.

"See? *My client* wants me here as well. For God's sake, I'm his adviser after all." The way he'd said *my client* aggravated Jessica to no end. She'd been here first, and Francesco could stand to show her even a shred of respect and courtesy. Who did he think he was?

She stood up, realizing she had nothing else to say. She knew Elias was in Giulianis' back pocket and had missed her chance. *This idiot of a gangster was pulling his strings just at the right time after the death of Davide. The New York Harbor might have to wait until we've wiped out that Giuliani egotistical bullshit for good.*

"Well, unfortunately, you came right when we were finished."

"Is that so? Because I thought I heard you still talking when I came inside."

"Yes, we will not be able to find common ground on a deal, so I will visit Mister Elias some other time with a better offer." She looked at Elias and he lowered his head, staring at the ground.

"Elias, don't let this young lady scare you. After all, I made you who you are today. I'm here to help you out. You are like family to me, old man." Francesco said not looking at him. His eyes were still focused on the Lombardi girl.

"You should feel lucky, Elias for having such a competent counselor like Mr. Francesco. I'd pay a lot of money for someone who is so *caring* to his clients." She didn't look at Elias either. Francesco and Jessica were side-talking one another.

The old man opened his mouth but he was interrupted by Francesco.

"By the way, Jessica, you could hire me as your counsel. If you have issues that require a man's touch, if you understand my meaning?" Francesco teased Jessica, grabbing his hat and returning it to his head.

"Well, that depends on the price, Mr. Francesco. I'm just a lowly lawyer trying to make a living." Their dialogue was theatrical, both speaking with hints of mockery and condescension. It was all to outsmart each other, in the presence of poor Elias, who was sitting in his chair, silent and spectating.

Finally, Jessica was ready to leave. She grabbed her purse. "I should get going."

"Elias, you don't need anything else, right?" Francesco asked and Elias shook his head, stunned.

"I will walk you outside, Miss Jessica." Jessica was disgusted, tired of his mock flattery, but she nodded as she headed towards the exit.

Francesco followed her to the steps of the entrance. It was almost 11 AM and the sun was already blazing. A few minutes outside and they both were sweaty. The stench of the seawater mingled repugnantly with the smell of petrol and fish. Francesco watched Jessica as she waited for him to say something.

"What do you drink?"

"It's 11 am. What is wrong with you?"

"A glass of wine helps move the day forward, doesn't it?"

"Wine? Ugh. If you are going to drink, at least drink something decent."

"Decent? Like the shitty whiskeys, the Irish sell around here?"

"No, like Gin that they sell around here."

"You've got to be kidding me. Gin?"

"Yeah, what's wrong with that?"

"It tastes like piss."

"Not everyone has a taste for the finer things, Francesco, that's life."

"Well, clearly, you have yet to try the finer things, but I'd be glad to introduce you. I know a good Italian pub nearby. Come join me so we can talk... about business?"

Was this Italian man hitting on her or was he just spying on the Lombardis? Either way, Jessica was prepared and viewed it as an opportunity to get as much information on the Giulianis as she could. *Spy for a spy*, she thought. Jessica wouldn't like his company, or that's what she kept telling herself. The man was conceited and flamboyant. *But what if he didn't have anything to offer, what would happen next?* This is what bothered Jessica; the unknown with this cocky mobster. She was afraid both of wasting time, and possibly enjoying herself. She fixed her sunglasses and glanced at the dock.

"Ok, I guess. Why not?"

Francesco wasn't asking her out, but this came about so naturally that it surprised him. How did the conversation end up here? Now, they're about to go drinking at 11 in the morning. Francesco couldn't take his offer back now. Not that he wanted to, but Francesco was making up an excuse in his head why he should. He told himself he'd go out with her only to learn more about the deal the Lombardis wanted with Elias. His charm, he believed would convince her to tell him everything.

"Follow me," he said smiling and offering her his arm as he led the way. She politely obliged, linking her arm with his, and decided the hot summer sun was the cause for her feeling warm inside.

* * *

For fifteen minutes in the blazing sun, they walked until they reached their destination. During the walk, they remained silent, their minds strategizing, each devising the perfect plan for extorting information out of one another; It was amusing, nevertheless.

Now, they were outside an old, dusty pub whose sign outside read, *Open from 8 a.m. to 11 p.m.* There were still chairs stacked on top of the tables. The wooden sign outside gave an old feeling to it. The words wrote in Italian on the top of the sign read, *Castello di Vino,* meaning the Castle of Wine.

Jessica gave way for Francesco to lead the way. She stopped for a moment. *Was this really a pub? It looks so old. Is he setting me up?* Francesco turned around troubled by Jessica's halt. "Is everything ok, my dear?"

"Yeah, it's just...It looks like someone's torture chamber." Francesco laughed like someone who was snorting cocaine.

"What? Why are you laughing?" Jessica was annoyed by Francesco's childish attitude.

"Dear, if I wanted you dead, you wouldn't have left that port in one piece. Hey, let's just say it's a little old-fashioned. Relax." He headed inside and for some reason, she believed him Any normal person would have freaked out, but his insistence had calmed her. She chalked it up to the Giuliani's smooth talking. That was the world these two mobsters chose to live in. A world where you should always look over your shoulder. Despite her reservations, Jessica followed Francesco inside.

Entering, she tasted the fresh smell of wine entering her throat. It was a very sweet and familiar aroma that reminded her of back home in Italy. All her negative feelings evaporated as she walked further inside. The place was dusty, with just a few shafts of light piercing through the rafters, creating a dark ambiance. But this was no torture room. It looked more like a drug shop. Francesco went to the bar and grabbed a stool. Jessica stayed still, examining the place which truly was traditionally designed. There were wooden barrels on the walls, stained glass windows and instead of conventional lighting, elaborate chandeliers hung from the ceiling. There was a grand piano on one side of the seating area, with a cello to keep it company. The pub looked as if it belonged in another era. It was charming to find something so beautifully out of place in the center of New York.

The keeper stood behind the bar waiting. The moment he saw Francesco, he hastily tried fixing his messy black hair and ruffled white shirt. The man was clean-shaven and appeared to be in his forties. He resembled a bartender in the medieval time period with his choice of clothing.

"Signore Francesco! Che piacevole sorpressa! It's been a while since you visited Castello."

"Ciao Federico! It's been a while indeed."

"E questa la tua ragazza?" the man asked.

"No, Sono una amica!" Jessica hissed. "She's Italian, Federico and no, she isn't my girlfriend," Francesco laughed loudly. Federico lowered his head, embarrassed. He pretended to clean a wine glass. "This is Miss Jessica Lombardi." Jessica was smiling, waiting to see the owner's reaction but on guard just in case she was being set up. Federico's eyes widened and his mouth was agape in surprise. The man couldn't hide his thoughts as he looked at Francesco and then back at Jessica, back and forth, processing.

"Maria Vergine! This is something I never expected to see in my entire life." He wiped the sweat from his forehead.

Jessica and Francesco looked at each other, laughing at Federico's comment. The whole thing felt like a rehearsed prank, but it wasn't. For this moment, these two had forgotten about their plans for their respective families. They were about to have a good time, staring at each other with all these customs passing through their minds. One stare lasted more than typical; a friendly one and they were lost in its moment.

The long stare was interrupted by the Frederico's voice. "Cosa ti va da bere signorina?"

"A gin with tonic would be fine," Jessica said as she took her eyes off Francesco, acting as if she was looking for something inside her purse.

"Gin? We have the best wine in New York and you chose gin?" Frederico stuttered as he grabbed a bottle of gin below the bar's counter.

"I don't like wine." Jessica closed her purse and Frederico became suspicious.

"How can someone who's Italian not enjoy vino?" Federico poured the gin inside a crystal glass.

"Don't mind her Federico, some of us just don't have a great taste." Jessica ignored Francesco, looking at the place's design. "I'll take the usual." Francesco sat on the wooden stool as Frederico had first served the drinks before carrying a few tables out front for them to sit. The area inside the pub's center was more comfortable and welcoming.

Francesco turned towards Jessica with his glass of wine raised. "A toast, before we discuss business."

Jessica raised her glass of gin. "A toast then," she said calmly, almost matching his tone.

"To our family businesses!"

"To the Lombardis then!"

"I was thinking, to the Giulianis but yes, to the Giuliani and Lombardis as well!"

"By the end of the year, the Lombardis will run New York, you know that, right?"

"Oh, I'm not so sure about that but only time will tell."

"Do you want to place a wager?"

"Betting on such things would be considered theft. I don't want to take your money."

"Oh! Where does that certainty come from?"

"Let's say I have faith in my family's business."

A small pause followed as they took sips. Francesco put his glass on the bar's counter and came back over.

"How come I've never seen you around? A pretty Lombardi girl, messing around with my Giuliani business, I'm sure I'd have noticed."

"I was out of town for the past ten years."

"Out of town? Where were you? If I may ask."

"Italy."

"Back home?"

"Yes, I wanted to do something with my life; I wanted to help our family, so I got my degree there in law."

"A woman of business and educated. That is rather impressive, I must say."

"What about you Francesco? Have you spent all your life here?"

"Admittedly, yes. I don't travel to Italy a lot. Born and raised here in New York. But I definitely have brought our family business to its peak."

"Oh? How so? Do you have a degree in marketing?"

"Haha, you're funny. No, I've learned the business the hard way. But, unlike you, I know exactly how these part-nerships work."

"Maybe, you underestimate me, Francesco."

"I don't think I do. Today's accomplishments speak for themselves. We retained the Harbor while your family got nothing in return!"

Jessica turned and took a sip of her drink. She tried holding back her smile, but it was difficult. Now, she realized Davide, on his deathbed, had decided to talk. That's how Francesco was able to control Elias and maintain his family's interests at the Harbor. All this young woman had to do was to keep Francesco talking. She was almost finished her gin when turned back to Francesco putting on a fake look of sorrow.

Francesco hadn't realized his mistake of talking too much. He was amused by Jessica's look and suspected she was faking. Yet, Francesco continued to smile as he ordered more wine. The word "Triumph" was written all over Francesco Giuliani's face.

"It's ok, Jessica. Next time."

"I'm new to the business and still learning the ropes. What can I say?"

"One step at a time, my dear. One day, maybe, and just maybe, the Lombardis will reach the Giulianis."

Jessica nodded softly drinking the last of her gin. All she needed to do was to leave this arrogant capo feeling victorious, so she got up suddenly. "Thanks for the drink but I think we'll have to reschedule this little meeting of ours to another time," she said looking at her watch.

"Why the sudden rush to leave?" Jessica smiled as she went between the tables and chairs looking backward.

"I have to take care of something. You know, family business." She passed by Federico standing over by the entrance. "Nice meeting you, Federico."

"Nice meeting you too, Signora Jessica," Federico said bowing slightly.

Francesco sat alone, in his hand was a glass of wine half-full as he looked at Federico confused. Federico just shrugged, scratching his half-bald head. Francesco didn't expect for the Lombardi girl to leave just like that. He learned zero from her. Yet these few moments away from the job made him smile. He finished his wine as calmly as he could. The young Italian enforcer was rising in rank within the New York's mafia circles but on the inside, he needed something from this cute Lombardi girl. He figured he still *needed* to know more and was determined to meeting her again.

6

THE INTERROGATION

The FBI

Special Agent Thomas Miller walked through the morning crowds of the streets of New York, heading towards the NYPD 5th Precinct. He left Quantico in a hurry, leaving his favorite sunglasses and umbrella behind. Thomas opened his pack of smokes and found a single crumbled one at the bottom. He moaned throwing the packet in the street. At the nearest street vendor, Thomas grabbed the newspaper and waited in line. He sighed, relieved that there was no mention of Davide Baldinotti's murder. The last thing he wanted was the press blowing the story out of proportion. In the past, they botched a few of his cases in court after a few pieces of sensitive evidence had been leaked prematurely.

"Hey, bud! Give me a pack of cigarettes and a hot cup of coffee."

"You got it. Coming right up."

Agent Miller set off to the police precinct, overlooking everything around him from traffic congestion, Chinese storefronts, and taxi drivers' horns beeping. All he wanted was to enjoy his hot coffee and a cigarette before being briefed on today's hodgepodge of cases.

Twenty minutes passed by and Agent Miller had arrived at the NYPD 5th Precinct, a discolored building stained from years of fossil fuels burned throughout the city. Seeing its dirty windows and cops coming out every minute or so, Miller felt lucky he was working in DC, at Quantico. Thomas walked slowly inside as the double doors squeaked. The place was in chaos with officers shouting, telephones ringing and a criminal trying to escape. The suspect ended up on the ground, moments later, tackled by three policemen.

Thomas walked to the reception, finding a young blonde lady talking on the phone. She lifted her hand, requesting for Thomas to wait another minute. Then, she lowered, covering her mouth but Thomas still heard her.

"Yes, sweetie. Of course, I'll cook for you today." The young woman played charmingly with her hair. "Oh, you're such a charmer." Thomas rolled his eyes and placed his hands on her desk and the woman knew the man was growing impatient. "I have to go, sweetie, talk to you later." She hung up and quickly shifted to Agent Miller.

"How may I help you?"

"Was that a professional call, Miss… Claire?" Thomas leaned in checking her name tag.

"Hmm, is that your concern, Mister?"

"Thomas Miller, FBI. We spoke earlier," Thomas said, showing her his badge.

"I am so sorry, sir. I didn't know it was you. I—"

"I don't care about your love life, Claire. I really don't. I'm here for one reason." He lifted a finger to his lips signaling her to keep quiet.

"I'm here to lead the investigation into the murder of Davide Baldinotti. Now, where is my desk?"

"Next to the interrogation room on the left, Agent Miller. Captain Hughes was briefed on your arrival early this morning."

"By the way, is Captain around?"

"No, sir. He called out sick today."

"Where can I find Officer Woods?"

"He called out sick, sir, too," Claire said after going through the morning call-outs.

Thomas pinched the bridge of his nose, sighing.

"For God's sake, does anyone actually work around here? At least, tell me where's Officer Howards?"

"I think I saw him going down to the canteen, sir.

Is there anything else, sir?"

* * *

Thomas left without saying anything further. Even as a

smoker, the precinct's cigarette odor made him nauseous. Covering his face, he entered the canteen, where the reek was even worse. The sound of cutlery clinking, food workers yelling, and loud conversing of the officers on duty was unwelcome. Most of the commotion was coming from five officers at one table. Thomas' eyes watered from the cigarette smoke in the air which appeared to cover every square inch of the rec area. Even the shafts of sunlight coming from the windows couldn't pierce the thick veil of smoke.

"Jonathan Howards" Agent Miller shouted, once inside. Every policeman and woman in the lunchroom turned towards the shouting agent.

"That's me" Jonathan yelled out from the back table. "Can I help you, pal?" The officer walked towards Miller and the agent inspected him as he closed the distance between them.

"Come with me, please." Thomas turned and headed for the entrance, expecting Howards to follow.

"Why would I do that, Mister?"

"Thomas Miller, FBI."

"Where's your badge, pal?" the mouthy officer chided.

"You have 30 seconds to move your ass to the interrogation room, or I'll be the one dragging it."

Jonathan stood there for a second, incredulous. He was annoyed but obeyed the ranking officer and followed. Thomas opened his makeshift office as a feeling of dizziness descended upon him seeing the mess left behind;

stacked-up boxes with files thrown over all over the place. On the desk, the only things not covered in dust, were Officers' Howards and Woods files as well as the photos of the evidence taken from the Baldinotti crime scene. Thomas rubbed his eyes and opened Jonathan's file. He spent 45 minutes looking over the reports. Officer

Howards reached the scene at 10:05 a.m., along with Officer Wood. They'd been patrolling the neighborhood when they came upon two dead guards in the front and immediately called it in. They didn't wait for back up. Then, they headed inside, to the second floor where they found a third guard and then Davide's body. Backup arrived with the forensics department quickly in tow, to collect evidence from the crime scene. After that, they immediately headed back to the precinct and filed their report at 10:45 am. Howards' report nearly matched Wood's.

No discrepancies that appeared glaring, but Agent Miller kept reading the report over and over feeling something wasn't right. His thoughts were interrupted by a light knock on the door.

"Come in." In came a woman, in her thirties, with brunette hair, holding an envelope. Thomas raised his head.

"Garcia. I see you're still trying to fit in a man's world." Thomas took a sip of his coffee. The officer brushed her black pants and fixed her white shirt, standing up straighter, proudly.

"Good morning to you too, sir. Welcome back," she

responded as adjusted her badge, pinned to the left of her button-down.

"What's in the envelope?"

"The coroner's report, sir." She walked forward, placing the envelope on the desk.

"Anything new?" Thomas opened it, giving it a quick glance.

"Nothing much, sir. Forensics say the bullet entered from close range directly in the middle of the forehead. This definitely was premeditated."

"It says here the time of death was around 10 AM. How come?" Thomas kept going back and forth over the report with skepticism.

"We know that already, sir. The timing suggests the gunman knew everyone would be out working."

"No, Garcia, we don't know. That's conjecture." Agent Miller got up grabbing files from off his desk.

"I'm not getting you, sir?" Garcia crossed her arms behind her back, looking worried.

"If you can't figure this one out Garcia, I won't bother explaining." Miller scoffed.

She stood as Agent Miller passed by her heading towards Interrogation.

* * *

Jonathan sat in a wooden chair, in front of a rusty table, staring at himself in the mirror. The door opened and

Agent Miller entered the room, taking a seat across while laying out the case files.

"Look, pal, you might be FBI or whatever but I have a job to do and it's called locking up fucking crooks. Something, you *desk guys* back at the *Bureau* don't see to have much experience in."

Jonathan slammed his fists on the table. "Why the fuck am I here anyway?" Thomas sighed and lit a cigarette, blowing out some smoke, which only added to his angry appearance

"I have work to do, so can we speed this up." Jonathan crossed his arms.

"So, do I. So, what time did you arrive at the Baldinotti crime scene?" Thomas opened the envelope with Howards' report.

"It says it in the report."

"Yes, but I'm asking you." Thomas' eyes were glued on the report, sifting through the pages, hoping to catch Jonathan Howards in a lie. The officer smiled.

"10:05 AM"

"Who checked his watch for the time?" Thomas took a drag of his cigarette, letting the ashes fall.

"What?"

Thomas looked up at the officer, with his eyebrows raised, staring at Jonathan straight in the eyes. Jonathan buttoned up his shirt and then wiped his sweaty hands on his trousers. There was a muteness in the room as Thomas kept staring waiting for Howards' answer.

"Wh—what do you mean?"

"Who checked his watch? It's a simple question."

"No one. We were on the scene, saw the bodies and ran inside to make sure that the scene was clear. The gate was open and when we got upstairs, one guard and Davide were lying there dead," Jonathan stated quickly but was having trouble swallowing.

"10:05 is a very exact time, don't you think?" Thomas opened Wood's report.

"Could be but, of course, we double checked it once we got inside the car, before calling headquarters."

"Yes, that's what I was asking. Who checked the watch?"

"It was Terry. After checking, we went back upstairs to the top floor to see if there were any suspects still around." Jonathan smiled closing the report and resting his hands on the table.

"Wood's report says he called it in from the radio. Not the car."

Jonathan's eyes widened as he crossed his legs, straightening himself again.

"He might have checked his watch. Look, pal, I don't remember all the specifics, okay?"

Thomas closed the report and tossed his cigarette on the ground.

"So, this is your formal statement that you don't remember the details?"

Jonathan stayed silent, only tapping his foot on the ground. "Who's paying you, Jonathan? The Lombardis or the Giulianis?"

"You're out of order, pal! Where's your damn proof?"

"It took me less than an hour to find out, so you really think I'll have trouble getting *proof* by the end of your fucking shift?" Jonathan sat with his mouth agape at the agent, incredulous that he was so cocky and rude all at the same time. Beads of sweat visibly formed at his brow and he swallowed hard, in frustration that they'd been so careless with the facts.

He said nothing as Agent Miller got up and took his files

"Try reaching out to your friend, Terry, so you can get your stories straight. You're dismissed."

* * *

Agent Miller opened the door in the rear which led directly to his office. Thomas plopped down in a creaky old chair, tossing the files atop the desk. Dust billowed out around him and he coughed, annoyed that his *office* was really an old, neglected office, that really needed renovations.

Moments later, Agent Garcia entered holding a notepad.

"Are Woods and Howards really getting paid by the crime families?"

"For sure."

"How can we prove that?"

"Weren't you taking notes, Garcia?"

Garcia glanced down at her notepad and put it behind her back.

"Umm, yes sir."

"Cut the crap and hurry up with the full forensics report."

"Yes, sir." Garcia said, turning on her heel.

Thomas reclined back, pondering as he viewed the busy street. The more officers the mobsters buy, the sloppier things get, and the easier it is to find a slip-up; and this time he found one. If he could break Jonathan, Terry would eventually spill, and he'd have a name. Just a single name would be enough to take down one family. If one goes, the others will start snitching to cut a deal. It was the domino-effect playing out inside Thomas' thoughts and he believed he might have pushed the first tile.

A loud knock sounded and then another uniformed officer entered. Thomas turned around, inspecting him. His suit medals revealed he was the captain of the precinct.

"Entering without a response is a little weird, don't you think, Captain?"

"Cut the bullshit, Agent Miller? I don't have time for your antics."

"With all due respect, sir, the Baldinotti murder is now with the Feds. That means you got me once again."

"You can't just stroll in here, harassing my officers without my permission."

"Okay, I'm sorry, Captain." Miller raised his hands defensively.

"So, I made hope I made myself clear. Next time, you inform me before harassing my officers. They work for me, chain of command and all."

"Well, the next will be Terry Wood and after him, every single cop in this precinct who's getting paid by the Italians."

"How dare you come in here from your plush desk in DC and accuse my officers of misconduct? I gave you a fucking office, our resources and you throw dirt on my deputies?"

"You need to cut the bullshit, Captain. If you believe that your officers are as sinless as babies, you are dumb as shit or you're involved too. Honestly, I don't know which scenario is worse."

"Hurry up with your case and never set foot in my precinct again. Do you hear me, Miller? Fucking cocksucker." Hughes left slamming the door behind him.

"I get that a lot." Thomas moaned, pinching the bridge of his nose and turning around, descending once again into his thoughts.

7

A FAMILY REUNION

The Lombardi Family

Jessica was on her way to the Lombardi Mansion and it was a two-hour ride through New York's dreaded traffic. Throughout, Jessica didn't speak, staring at the animation; attorneys like her running in and out the courthouses, construction workers repairing streets and street vendors yelling while customers were shopping. Jessica's facial expression resembled a little girl who'd dropped her ice cream. While everyone appeared to be happy, Jessica was returning home defeated. A defeat from a man who didn't possess a college degree, a man born and raised in a household of those who were stuck in the old Italian ways.

Jessica started considering if she was cut out for this but knew she wouldn't go down that easily. She would refocus and come back stronger, proving to her father she was smarter than her brother Giovanni or anyone else on her father's payroll.

"How did it go Miss Jessica?" the driver said, with a quiet, but gravelly voice.

"How did it go what?" Jessica snapped at the driver. She hadn't meant for her response to come out so harsh, but she was still fired up about the Francesco getting in her way.

"The job."

"How does my father allow a driver to ask questions?"

"We've been friends for ages."

"Ok, but your job is to only drive the car."

"I see you are upset. I believe the job wasn't done. I've been around long enough to tell."

"If you know so much, how come you ended up being a driver?"

"I like driving."

"Yeah, whatever. Just stop meddling in my business or we'll see how much you enjoy driving without your hands."

Paul smiled knowing Jessica didn't have that kind of power yet. He didn't want any problems, so he obliged and turned on the radio. The rest of the journey resumed in silence and Jessica gazed out the window. After the traffic lightened up a bit, they finally reached the western suburbs of New York, not far from the Lombardi Mansion . The neighborhood was quiet, and a few of the elderly residents were out taking their dogs for a walk. Some waved at Paul and Jessica as they drove by. Paul greeted, nodded and smiled while Jessica pretended they didn't exist.

The car reached the Lombardi Mansion and Jessica got out, giving her home a long stare while Paul drove inside the garage. Jessica gaped in the shadow of the stone giant that towered three stories over her. Even though she'd spent plenty of time in the mansion, it's beauty and grandeur was never lost on her. In contrast to the Giuliani Mansion , the Lombardi's was constructed with Victorian Age details to its architecture. Its dark red brick walls reminded her of the cheap summer dresses her mother had bought when she was little and Jessica hated them. The wooden stairs in the front, Jessica remembered she used to greet her father when he came home from work. Those same stairs, now she had to climb up, in a state of disappointment. Jessica took a deep breath and started escalating, taking off her sunglasses and placing them inside her purse. She cleared her throat and opened the front door when she heard her mother calling from the dining room.

"You're back already sweetie?" Jessica was deaf to her mother's question, ignoring and nimbly going to her room.

She locked the door and threw her handbag on the chair and lied down, staring at the ceiling of paper stars she used to make as a child. Those stars were the only thing that helped her sleep at night. Jessica kept staring, reflecting on the day's events. She closed her eyes and the same memory played over and over— a man in a white suit barging in Elias' office and taking her deal, thus ruining her. Jessica tensed feeling exhausted but couldn't sleep right away. Hurt and defeat were cooking up her brain. She knew she had to do something about this man and didn't want her father to take care of it. She had to do something but now she was finally asleep.

* * *

A faint knock on the door woke her. Jessica opened her eyes and sprang up, worried. The room was darkened and she wondered what time it was. She heard the knock again and reached for the light on her nightstand —7 p.m. She'd overslept, feeling groggy and only wanted to lie down for another hour.

"Who is it?" Jessica said hoarsely, clearing her throat.

"We're having dinner, sweetheart." It was her father. Her eyes beamed with joy at the sound of his voice but that joy quickly turned into worry. How could she face him after today's mess?

"I'll be there in a sec." Jessica tidied up, took a deep breath and came downstairs. Mixed emotions were clouding her mind and the stress got worse as she was approaching the living room where she heard multiple conversations. She counted four different voices blending in with the low hum of the T.V. Jessica stopped at the living room door. Apart from her parents, she observed her grandmother and brother, Giovanni. Jessica stood there, seeing everyone eating burgers and fries from her favorite restaurant, Burger King. Her grandmother, the usual guest of honor, was relaxing on a burgundy leather recliner, enjoying a glass of wine with a slim cigarette. Dressed in old Italian black attire, she matched perfectly with the couch. Jessica had never seen the old woman eat. Her father, mother, and brother were enjoying *Married with Children* on the new TV.

When Jessica came inside, everyone turned.

"Finalmente, Nipotina!" her grandmother shouted trying to get up from the recliner. Her legs were shaking as she pushed upwards to greet her granddaughter.

"Don't get up, grandma. It's ok." Jessica rushed and kissed her on the cheeks.

"If I don't greet my granddaughter properly, who will?" The old woman stood up and hugged Jessica tightly.

"I missed you, Nipotina!" Jessica released herself, standing playfully in front of her grandmother, feeling like a little child when she did that. "Abbiamo molto da discuterem," said the old woman taking a sip of wine.

"Yes, we do." Jessica smiled, agreeing they had much to discuss.

"Dai Mamma. You'll talk to her later. Come greet your papa, Jessica," Michael stood up and Jessica felt his big belly pressing against her as his enormous hands lifted her up from the ground.

"Michael Lombardi, don't talk to your mother like that!" The old woman replied back.

"Dad, stop doing that," Jessica said trying to breathe.

"What? I haven't seen my daughter since morning." Michael slowly let his daughter leave his embrace.

Michael went back to his place when Giovanni stood and hugged his sister. "How was your day, little one?" he said smoothly and smiling. Jessica hugged him back and kissed him on the cheek. "The usual."

Jessica then leaned in and kissed her mother on the cheeks looking around. She gathered the courage to speak to her father and said, "Dad, can we talk for a sec?"

"Yes, sweetheart," he said getting up.

"Oddio! Michael why you leave your food?" Jessica's grandmother complained.

"Mamma, please relax. You're killing me," Michael said as he followed Jessica. Jessica closed the living room door behind hearing her grandmother's swearing in Italian.

The two walked inside her father's office and Michael took a seat behind his old mahogany desk while Jessica kept standing. The office had an intimidating appearance. The bookcases and the desk were lit only by the desk lamp. It was a place for someone who was fully concentrated on business. Jessica only came to it when she'd done something bad when she was younger.

"So, what is it, my dear?" Her father's facial expression turned serious.

"I screwed up, Papa." Jessica stuttered leaning on the wall.

"I know."

"H—how?"

"If we'd closed the deal with Elias, I think I'd know by now."

"I'm really sorry."

"You should be. That was a backbreaker, Jessica."

Jessica gasped feeling her eyes watering.

"I told you your brother could handle this, but you insisted."

"Dad, it's not my fault. The Giulianis knew ahead of time."

"Of course, they did! They killed Davide to get the Harbor. You think that idiot wouldn't talk?"

"But dad—"

"Let me finish!" Michael raised his voice. "I care about this city as much as I care about my family, Jessica. I can't let anyone get in our way, especially those barbarians who still believe they live in prehistoric Italy. This is New York and I will take care of it."

As Michael was practically yelling, Jessica couldn't hold in tears anymore. A teardrop slid down her cheek, which she quickly wiped off, hoping her father wouldn't notice. Michael paused.

"Look. You're new to this profession, I get it. Maybe you should focus your energy on what you are good at and help us with the legal stuff."

"Papa, I don't just want to be your lawyer."

Michael groaned, pondering what to do. "I'll give you one chance at a later time, but Jessica, I won't tolerate another mess. Otherwise, I'll let Giovanni handle the business from now on."

Jessica nodded heeding her father's words. She turned around and opened the door, quickly running upstairs to her bedroom. Jessica failed her father once again; the same way she'd done when she moved to Italy for her education instead of staying home as he'd advised , after that when she didn't finish her classes on time, and finally, when she didn't find love when he proposed that she marry Geno, a longtime ally's son. Jessica slammed the door and couldn't control her grief any longer. She stretched out on the floor, crying. It wasn't her father's fault; it was hers and hers entirely.

Jessica positioned herself on her purple rug; the one she used to play on, with her toys, when she was just a little girl when her father was innocent to her. Those moments of delight often helped calm her. She tried remembering the happy moments of her short young life but was interrupted by the footsteps climbing the stairs. A soft knock and Jessica responded sniffling,

"Who is it?"

"Nipotina, Grandma's leaving." Jessica rushed towards the door, opening it quickly. Her grandmother was holding her walking cane. Jessica hugged her, with tears still streaming down her cheeks.

"Please don't," she whispered as she squeezed her grandmother's hand.

"Oh, I can't stay the night. Your grandmother is an old woman now."

Jessica hugged her tightly. "Can you stay just a little longer?" She pleaded with eyes as big as saucers.

Her grandmother considered this for a moment and finally said, "Tutto per mia nipote"

"Grazie!" she said, clasping her hand together, genuinely happy her grandmother had agree to stay.

"Why are you crying, nipotina?"

"Nothing."

"If you want me to stay, you must fidati di, you must trust me."

"It's dad."

"Quel figlio di puttana Michael, I swear I'll cut his tongue."

"No, please."

"Who does he think he is insulting my nipotina like that?"

"He didn't. He's right."

"What did he say now? Non sei capace to run the business, that Giovanni is more fitted? Hah!"

"H—how do you know?"

"He is always like that! That bastard of a son. Don't listen to him."

"What should I do?"

"Now that you are grown woman, seguine il tuo cuore. Never forget that."

Jessica hugged her grandmother again, taking a breath of joy and relief. "Thank you."

"Don't thank me! If I can't help, who can? Let the fat man bark Che abbaia non morde!"

"One's bark is worse than one's bite. It's been years since you told me that."

"Rest now, nipotina. Have a good breakfast tomorrow and all will be fine."

Jessica smiled and kissed her grandmother on the cheek. "See you soon."

"Oh, I'll be here every day." her grandmother winked and turned, leaving Jessica. Jessica's confidence was boosted by her grandmother, the loveliest woman in the world. Even her mother couldn't comfort her like the old woman. Jessica lied down, staring back up at the paper stars, wondering what task her father might give her next time.

8

***

WRITTEN CONFESSIONS

Terry Woods

To Agent Thomas Miller:

I was recently informed about your arrival in New York and the case you are working on. I was informed by my partner Jonathan Howards, that I am your only suspect and lead in the Davide Baldinotti case.

I cannot do this anymore. I want to confess but the moment I do, I will be full of lead by some certain individuals. I want to confess what my partner and I had done and I want to do it as soon as possible.

I've wanted to do this for a long time but our precincts and captains can't offer me safe passage.

You, Agent Miller, can. You can take me out of this swamp I've been living for the past two years.

I want to schedule a meeting with you, somewhere private but I want you to have a deal in place. I want immunity and witness protection. I am alone in this world; I have no family or friends so it would be easier for you to do that.

I want immunity for my partner Jonathan Howards as well. He wants to be put into witness protection along with me.

I'd like to meet at 20 Mott St, 9:00 PM, Sunday in the alleyway.

Please Agent Miller, come alone with a written deal I can sign. If you prosecute us, we will die and will be dead the moment we reach the courthouse. If we somehow survive that, we won't be so lucky in prison.

I implore you, keep this letter a secret. For the good of Jonathan, myself, and your case against the families.

Sincerely yours,
Terry Wood

9

CLEANING HOUSE

The Giuliani Family

Francesco sat silently in Castello di Vino sipping on a glass of wine while Federico was cleaning, getting the pub ready for opening.

"Tutto okay? " Fredrico asked, looking up from his sweeping.

"Yes."

"You don't seem right today."

"I'm fine." Francesco said curtly, taking another sip.

"Your thoughts are wandering."

"You could say so."

"Does it wander somewhere particular?"

"No, not really."

"Maybe to that bella ragazza?" Fredrico prodded.

"The girl is a Lombardi, Federico." Francesco sighed.

"Lombardis are not pretty?"

"They are. They really are." Francesco said, rubbing his brow.

"So, what's the problem? She seems inteligente. Smart."

"Not mafia bright, but definitely smart." He chuckled, swirling the red wine in his glass.

"I would ask her out if I were you."

"I have a business to run Federico. It's not all that simple."

"So, what? You can't run famiglia *and* have a nice lady?"

"I really must focus right now."

"Famiglia will always trouble you, Francesco. Your father has a nice donna."

"It's hard to keep the empire in one piece. Harder than building it to begin with."

Federico shrugged. "You know better, I reckon." Federico grabbed a mop from behind the bar.

"I'm surprised you are not a vergine."

"Knock it off, Federico."

"You are?"

"No, I'm not. Why is this any of your business anyway?"

"I just want to see an old friend happy with famiglia. I want to be zio."

Francesco laughed. "You'd be a hell of a zio, Federico." Francesco finished his glass of wine, grabbed his hat and nodded. "I'll leave you clean up, this place looks like a mess," Francesco said walking towards the door.

"Vaffanculo, Francesco!" shouted Frederico as Francesco entered the busy street smiling. He looked around noticing everyone who walked by was. It made him happy, seeing New York like this. *Wish we lived like this more often*, he thought to himself as he waved a cab down.

* * *

An hour passed and Francesco was in the dining room, having a plate of Ciceri e Tria. He was alone, reflecting on the day's events. Another crisis had been averted for now, but he still had to do something about Elias and the Lombardis. Francesco was almost finished when the dining room door opened. His father, Luca walked in, dressed in a similar white suit as his son's. Francesco stood up and opened his arms, embracing the Don. "Father!" he shouted with excitement, clapping his father on the back. Luca hugged his son and kissed him on both cheeks. He then grabbed a seat at the end of the table smiling. The Don's face had a peaceful look in part because he knew his son's task was a success.

"How did it go?"

"Elias won't be a problem."

"Did he say anything to the Lombardi scumbags?"

"Nothing. I made sure of it."

"Who did they send?"

"A girl by the name of Jessica Lombardi. She claims to be a lawyer." Francesco said with a scoff, as he stirred his pasta. It wasn't entirely genuine, but he'd play the part his father required.

"Ah, Giovanni's younger sister."

"That's her! I didn't know Lombardi had a daughter."

"She wasn't raised in the business. How'd she do?"

"She was out of her element."

"Hmm, poor Michael. That probably cost him a fortune." Luca said,

"I could've handled Giovanni as well, father!" Luca looked at his son in displeasure. "That bastard Giovanni would be as easy as his sister".

"Son! Show some respect. They are our rivals, but they are still Italian family."

"I'm sorry, father."

"We have far more important issues right now to deal with, forget the Harbor."

"What happened?"

"I hear Terry Woods and Jonathan Howards plan to confess. What did you do, Francesco?"

"About Davide's death?"

"I just learned about the mess you left back at the Baldinotti Mansion ."

"I would have explained."

"But you didn't, Francesco." Luca raised his voice a bit. Francesco hushed, staring at the empty plate in front of him.

"Anyway, it doesn't matter how it happens. It should have been dealt with a long time ago."

"I'll take care of it, then."

"Yes, you will. Please, this time, don't leave a mess. We can't have more officers on our payroll."

"Why the hell do they want to confess all of the sudden?"

"There's a new FBI agent working our case. Our men in the precinct say he's determined to take us all down."

"But he won't."

"If those two want to confess, more will follow, you know that?"

"I do."

"We should make Terry and Jonathan examples. You get my drift, son. I trust you to take care of this."

"How will I reach them?"

"Jonathan will be taken care of. You just focus on Woods."

"Should we do it at his home?"

"Yes, he lives alone. Here's the address." Luca handed it to Francesco and patted his son on the back. "The driver is waiting for you out front." Luca got up and headed towards the kitchen. "I await the good news."

Francesco stared at the piece of paper.

This is a mess. First, Davide, and now these two rats. The Giulianis were losing grip of New York and Francesco wanted to do something about it; not letting a second to allow his family's empire crumble, he got up and rushed towards the front of the house where the vehicle was parked. Guillermo the driver leaned against the Crimson Fiat's door, finishing a cigarette.

"I was making bets with myself and you surprised me. Under 10 minutes!"

"Let's go."

"Ooh. Ready for business, Master Francesco?"

Francesco got inside as Guillermo shrugged flinging his cigarette on the street.

"Where to, Boss?"

"This address." Francesco handed Guillermo the crumpled piece of paper and lowered his hat, leaning back in his seat.

"Do we have any guns in the back?"

"Some heat. You know the usual."

"Smiths and Colts?"

"Yep."

"Excellente," Francesco said closing his eyes. He didn't want to think about anything that happened earlier including the Lombardi Girl. He didn't want to think of the Lombardis at all. His task was for his family; the Giulianis.

* * *

Terry Wood lived downtown, a few blocks from the 5th Precinct. Francesco spent the next 90 minutes in and out of asleep when the car stopped after Guillermo pulled the handbrake.

"We're here boss," Guillermo pushed the button to open the trunk. "This shouldn't take more than ten minutes. If you see anything suspicious, just go." Francesco warned as he opened the door and went to the trunk seeing a few 12 Gauges, a Colt M1911A1, and Smith and Wesson Model 19. Francesco looked around closely, noting that although the streets were busy, no one in sight paid him mind. This was why Francesco loved New York; it was every man for himself.

Francesco grabbed the Colt and headed towards Terry's apartment building. Examining the piece of paper again, he compared the mailboxes on the ground floor and saw Terry Woods' name written under Third Floor, Apartment 13C.

Francesco took the stairs up the old building reminiscing about having to live in a place like this when he was a child. The cooking gas coming out of the apartments, combined with dust and urine in the hallways made Francesco want to puke. He was glad his father bought the Giuliani Mansion away from the city. Yet, Francesco couldn't stop thinking about how this place was going to smell after Terry's passing. *In a shithole like this, it would take at least three days to find his body. Probably a neighbor tired of the rotten smell would call maintenance to check on the apartment. Or maybe this new FBI agent would just show up. Who knows? The only thing for sure was that Terry Woods would die today.*

Francesco walked cautiously, halting at every hallway entry, wishing not to be interrupted by some random cleaning lady or a curious neighbor. Now on the third floor, he went to check the numbers on the doors. At the end of the hallway was Apartment 13C. Francesco tapped up the steps lightly, but the sound echoed like church bells on the day of a funeral.

"Agent Miller?" Terry was standing behind the door and Francesco kicked it in, hitting plowing Terry over. Terry and the door both landed on the ground with a loud thud. A sliding metallic noise echoed through Terry's hollow apartment as his service revolver slipped a few feet away from him.

Francesco aimed at Terry's head while entering the room, never losing sight of the officer while pushing the door behind him close. The handle and lock had broken and that door would never function properly again.

Terry was lying on the ground, holding his bloody nose, letting out muffled screams of pain. "F—fuck." He tried crawling towards his gun as Francesco reached it first kicking it to the far corner of the room.

"I wouldn't do that if I were you."

"Why not? I'm already dead."

"Yes, you are."

"Fuck. I thought I'd get away with it."

"No one does Terry."

Terry stayed on the ground looking like a bloody mess with blood streaming down his face. Yet, he was smiling.

"No one?" Terry said trying to sit up.

"Stay there, Terry."

"Oh, what does it matter? Kill me while I'm down like a pig or kill me while I'm standing with honor."

"I said, stay down," Francesco said bearing the gun closer to Terry's temple.

"You're done. Fucking Giulianis," he said spitting out blood.

"You're done, Terry. You and your fucking pal, Jonathan."

Terry's eyes shrank as he lowered his head.

"I shouldn't have dragged him into this."

"But you did."

"He has a family."

"He should have thought of that sooner because we all do."

"I'm a loner. I wanted it all. Jonathan only wanted to protect his family."

"And he would have."

"May I pray, Francesco?"

"You should have done that the moment you sent that letter."

"I did and I'm not much of a good Christian, you know."

Francesco didn't speak, dropping his gun a little. Terry's eyes had the same peaceful look like Francesco's father's earlier in the morning.

"Agent Miller will get you, you know that. No one has had organized crime in this city on their heels like this man for over forty years." Terry spit out more blood.

"That's why he'll get you because you fucking old-timers are getting sloppy."

"The Giulianis will keep running New York."

"No, they will not. Your family is finished, and you know it. If Jonathan and I turned and Davide sided with the Lombardis, there will be more who will follow."

"We'll take care of it. No worries." Francesco assured him with a wink and smile, but there was no pleasure in his eyes.

"Keep killing and there will be no city to run. That is why they call you savages. Your way of running things is old-fashioned, bud."

"I'm sorry, Terry but you will be part of one of those old-time ways of running things."

"Get on with it. I had enough of this life."

Terry clasped his hands in one final, silent prayer. One gunshot echoed throughout the apartment. Francesco turned towards the door and didn't look back. He continued down the stairs to the outside of the apartment building. As he was descending the staircase, he heard steps from the third floor. Panicked, the neighboring doors were opening and closing like a symphony, followed by a loud old woman's scream. When Terry's body was discovered, Francesco was already in the front seat of the Fiat Spider. "We should hurry," he said, dropping the gun under the seat. Guillermo turned the key and the Fiat started like a spurred horse.

A clean job this time. No mess and no witnesses but it didn't feel like a success. It felt like the Giuilianis were now patching up a bag with too many holes. You don't fix the bag; you buy a new one or get rid of anyone poking it. That's what the family has been doing for the past weeks; cleaning house around town and matters were getting worse.

10

THE BLOODIED CELL

The FBI

It was around 14:00. Thomas was sitting amongst dozens of files spread out and documents piled up. He opened his pack of cigarettes finding only one left. In the ashtray nearby, it was full of half-smoked ones. Thomas groaned and took the last, then crumbled the package and threw it in the bin under his desk, a graveyard of cigarette packages and crumpled wads of paper.

He took a long drag, leaning back in the old, uncomfortable chair, looking at the broken fan hanging from the ceiling. Agent Miller held his cigarette for so long that he almost forgot he had lit up. He'd gotten lost in thought, *again.* One last drag and he put out the cigarette. The file on the Giuliani family was in front of him and it was smaller than the bills in his wallet. Thomas rubbed the back of his neck, resigning that he'd have to give the investigation his all if he wanted to make progress. He'd been about to scour the scant file, when his phone ringed.

"What?"

"Sir, it's Garcia."

"I know. What?"

"A letter arrived for you. I think you want to see it."

"Just bring it in here for Lord's sake."

"I just didn't want…"

Thomas hung up, looking back at the Giuliani file. His door creaked open and Garcia rushed in, putting the letter on Thomas' desk.

"What is this again?"

"A letter, sir."

"I know it's a damn letter, Garcia. When did it get here?"

"A few minutes ago, sir. It's from Terry Woods."

Thomas stared at Garcia as his jawbones dropped. He tore the envelope open, throwing it to the side while his rough hands were trembling. He rubbed his eyes and began reading. Garcia remained, looking at her boss, holding her breath.

After reading it, Thomas dropped it on the desk and practically leaped out of his desk chair, running towards the coat rack, and grabbing his trench coat. Garcia stood, confused by her boss' sudden departure, but she figured he wasn't surprised by the contents of the letter. Thomas Miller smiled.

"Sir, what's in it?"

"Terry Wood wants to confess, Garcia. He wants to

confess."

"Really?"

Thomas put on his coat and paused as if a hammer had just hit him in the head. His smile faded.

"Who brought in the letter, Garcia?"

"I…I don't know."

"Who brought it in?"

"Someone from the precinct."

"They're going to kill him. They know."

"What do you mean?"

"If we know, they know, Garcia."

"Who?"

"The people who pay Terry."

Garcia's pleasant emotion had left her face as quickly as Thomas'.

"What do we do?"

"We don't have time. Put Jonathan in a holding cell alone and meet me outside."

"In a holding cell? I thought we had nothing on him."

Thomas flashed the letter before the officer's eyes. Her jaw dropped once she'd finished reading it. She was confused as to what confession the other officers were planning on making, but realized they had reasonable doubt and could contain Jonathan for the time being.

"I'll explain on the way, Garcia. Just do what I ask for God's sake. Just once."

Thomas ran out of the precinct, pushing some officers out of his way. His only hope was getting to Terry before he got whacked. There was a homeless man being dragged in by officers struggling to get him inside a holding cell. The police captain watched him from the top of the staircase. Thomas paid the commotion no mind. The photos of Terry's file flashed in Thomas' subconscious as he hurried to his black service car in the front parking lot. He waited nervously for Garcia as she was lagging behind, carrying a pack of files, and almost dropping them. She got in, tidying up her hair, then sorting the files on her lap. The black service car dashed across the road, ignoring all the passing vehicles with the police siren blaring. Thomas' hands were hugging the wheel, his mind not completely on the road, but on his case which was even closer to being solved. Garcia's words were far away, like a voice coming from the depths of the ocean.

"Sir!" Garcia shouted three times, as Thomas narrowly missed hitting a little girl crossing the road.

"Please, slow down for God's sake," she said tightening her grip on the files.

Thomas looked at her and tried maintaining the speed, but still ignoring the traffic lights.

"Sir, why did we put Jonathan in holding?"

"To keep him safe."

"Safe from who?"

"The damn mobsters, Garcia."

For the next twenty minutes, Garcia imagined their achievement, how she and Agent Miller brought down New York's most notorious crime families, once and for all. Meanwhile, Thomas could only think about the likelihood of Terry's end. If it happened, he couldn't count on NYPD anymore; being that there'd be no one he could trust in the whole precinct.

Thomas parked outside Terry's building. He lowered the window seeing three police cars parked there already with flashing lights.

"Garcia, park the car." Thomas climbed out and headed towards the crowd gathered in front of the building.

The scene resembled a ring formed. Reporters and cameramen tried to get a good view of the crime scene along with others shouting. The officers barricaded the area, preventing anyone from entering, and compromising the crime scene.

Thomas pushed his way through towards the front line of the police officers. Cameras turned towards him while overlapping voices of reporters tried getting a statement, but Agent Miller heard nothing. His eyes were locked in and his breathing became difficult. The arrival of Terry's letter and now, his apparent execution only added to Miller's disappointment.

* * *

Meanwhile, the officers on the scene were finishing up surrounding the apartment building with police tape.

"Thomas Miller, FBI" Thomas took out his badge, showing it to an officer.

"Third Floor, Apartment C13," the officer said, tying

up the last strip of tape at the nearest streetlamp.

Thomas ducked under the yellow tape and passed through the crime scene. He walked with purpose but felt dread growing in him with each step. The building's tenants who were evacuated, watched outside.

Thomas reached Apartment C13, seeing the busted-down door. The forensics team was already inside and evidence was starting to be cataloged. The detectives and officers on the scene were talking but their voices were muted over by the sounds of the cameras' flickering.

Thomas entered, observing carefully, and quickly spotting Terry, lying still on the couch with a bullet through his temple, just like Davide Baldinotti.

"Sir?"

"Agent Miller, you mean," Thomas corrected coldly, holding his badge up with and iron grip, as if he was trying to crush it to pieces.

"Are you the lead agent on the case?"

"I am now."

"Officer Terry Wood was discovered about an hour ago."

Thomas pressed into his eyes, holding them shut as he took a deep breath.

"Any witnesses?"

"Only an old lady next door heard the gunshots but saw nothing."

"Any others who may have seen something? Was the receptionist when the gun was fired?"

"No, sir."

"Now, that's just great." Thomas walked closer to Terry's body and crouched, taking mental snapshots of the crime scene. Agent Miller didn't need the forensics team because he already knew what happened here. Terry was another dead end. There would probably be money stashed somewhere; money from the crime family payoffs, but nothing substantial.

"Catalog everything and bring the report to the 5th Precinct," he yelled walking outside the entrance where he saw Garcia coming off the elevator.

"Sir?"

"Not now, Garcia."

"What happened?"

"Nothing unexpected."

Garcia looked over Miller's shoulder at the crime scene.

"Time to question Jonathan."

"You think he'll confess?"

"After what happened today, does he have a choice?"

Thomas got back on the elevator. His eyes were glued to its tiles, unable to lift his head. Garcia followed and pressed the ground level button. The mood was dark and cold inside the elevator. Only the feeling of defeat loomed over the two agents. Thomas' hand was hurting from clenching his badge so long that it left a red mark, so he put it in his coat pocket. He almost welcomed the pain, because it made him feel alive, and something other than the pain of losing Woods. He wasn't particularly attached to the officer, but he needed him to bring down the two rival families, and now they'd set him back. Besides, he'd worked a couple of cases with Terry Woods, and he wasn't a bad guy. *A bad officer,* Thomas thought to himself, *but not a bad guy.*

Heading towards the service car, Agent Miller took out his pack of cigarettes, but it was empty.

"Garcia, do you smoke?"

"No, sir."

Thomas groaned as he climbed into the passenger side of the vehicle, signaling Garcia to drive. His hands were trembling and there was nothing he could do to calm himself. After the thirty-minute drive back to the precinct, Garcia parked outside, and Thomas quickly jumped out.

"Prepare Jonathan for interrogation, Garcia," Thomas said running towards the nearest newsstand, to get another pack of smokes.

He bought a pack along with a bottle of whiskey on sale at the liquor store outside the newsstand. As he ascended the stairs of the police precinct, he felt something was not right. No one was outside like when he first arrived. Not a single officer in sight. He opened the doors, freeing a stream of yells and screams. He handed Garcia his bottle and told her to take it to his office. Inside, he saw the station's officers running back and forth. The secretaries weren't at their stations and the police captain was surrounded by a crowd of uniformed officers as he shouted orders. No one appeared to be listening to him.

Thomas stood in the middle of the chaotic scene trying to process what happened. He looked around, trying to find anything. Garcia ran up to him.

"S…sir?"

"What the hell happened here, Garcia?"

"Mmm…"

"Just say something for God's sake!"

"J—Jonathan is dead, sir…" Garcia lowered her gaze, unable to look at Thomas.

Thomas rushed towards the holding cells, pushing the officers out his way. His eyes were on the Captain's. An expression of disgust as the Captain was looking for help, completely unable to keep the situation under control. Thomas pushed an officer, reaching the cell door, finding an ocean of blood flowing under his feet.

Thomas stepped inside; feeling vomit climbing up his throat from what he saw. Despite years on the job, this was something he never had to experience. The fresh smell of hot blood made his eyes water. Jonathan, still lying on the bench, with his throat gashed. On the floor, in the center of the cell, was the homeless man from earlier, holding a shiv covered in blood. His stomach was cut open, revealing his entrails. The cell resembled a horror movie. Thomas covered his nose and stepped back. He turned around to find Garcia.

"What the hell happened here?"

"The homeless man, sir. It appears he killed Jonathan?"

"They brought him in, for shoplifting, this morning."

"Didn't they search him for weapons?"

"They did sir but…"

"But what?" Thomas screamed. Every officer stopped what they were doing and turned towards Thomas. Silence surrounded as if the Jonathan's funeral had already begun. Thomas looked around and everyone including the Captain was waiting for him to speak.

"Listen here! I've seen plenty of scumbags in my life, but you are the fucking worst," Thomas eyes were red as pools of fire. The officers including the Captain gasped as murmurs began spreading across the station.

"You're the most worthless and incompetent bastards I've ever seen working on the beat since the invention of Hollywood." Thomas' voice echoed where it could be heard outside of the precinct.

"Two of your fellow officers were murdered today. Murdered by you!" He stared at the Captain. "Some of you are being paid by the mafia. *You* killed two men, ready to confess their mistakes. They took an oath to protect this city with some shred of dignity—to protect its citizens and you ended up killing two men who were willing to sacrifice their evil deeds for good ones." Thomas' hands were trembling and his breathing accelerated.

"And you, Dear Captain, are the worst piece of shit I have ever seen in charge of anything!" The Captain stared at the ground; his heavy shoulders and stiff body was rigid, but he said nothing.

"A whole precinct bought off by the fucking mafia

and you pretend to fucking care! I hope you all rot in hell." Thomas took a cigarette out from his pack.

"From now on, you're all off the case. Every last one of you, fuckers. I'll bring my own men to deal with your city's incompetence. Anyone holding even a single piece of paper will be considered an accomplice." Agent Miller left and headed to his makeshift office, slamming the door behind.

Everyone remained still including Garcia who was staring at Thomas' door with her mouth open. The agent's words stung. No one wanted to move but their silence was broken by the Captain, who stormed out first.

Meanwhile, Thomas Miller sat, crushing his cigarette on the pile of others in the ashtray and lit another. He took out the bottle of whiskey and poured himself some. He slammed his fists on the desk. *Another dead end.* His dominoes were not falling where he intended. Another dead end, thanks to his fellow policemen. Was this the system he is serving? Was this the system he swore to protect?

In an office opposite of Thomas', sat the Captain of the 7th Precinct holding a black telephone to his ears. He was tired of Miller's shit and wanted him out immediately.

"Lieutenant, we have a problem; Thomas Miller. He's forcing my hand. This cocksucker thinks he's running things up here, making accusations on my officers and myself that are baseless."

"Don't worry, Captain. I'll take care of it."

11

JUDE HAUL, LIFE INSURANCES

The Lombardi Family

Jessica was lying in her bedroom with only small rays of light finding its way through the closed shutters. She watched the small dust particles and tried counting them one by one. It was something she used to do back in Italy to help her sleep. She slept in her clothes and her eyes were red, exhausted from the lack of proper rest. A soft knock disturbed the quiet in her room.

"Come in." Her brother, dressed in a fine black suit, entered.

"Still asleep little one?"

"What is sleep?" she chuckled, wryly.

"Rough night again, huh?"

"Don't even mention it."

"I often wondered how you spend your sleepless nights."

"With frustration?"

"Sounds bad."

"Yeah, I don't have many options."

"Anyway, I'm here to cheer you up."

"You got me some Xanax, then?"

"I'd say something better."

"Sleeping pills?"

"I'm serious. Today's the day for a job."

"What job?"

"The one father wants you to do."

"The Haul?"

"Exactly."

"And why are you here, then?"

"Father wants me to make sure everything will go smoothly."

"Oh, so he doesn't trust me"

"He just wants to make sure we'll carry this out."

"We? It was *my* job. When did he tell you about it?"

"Five days ago? About the same time, he gave it you."

"He didn't lose a minute, did he?"

"You know father."

"When it comes to business, unfortunately, I do."

"Come on, it'll be fun. We don't hang out anymore anyways."

"If extorting people for money is your definition of hanging out, then I guess we need to catch up." Jessica got up brushing her hair. "I'll meet you downstairs in twenty minutes, okay?" she said, staring at the mirror.

"Okay, I'll have the car ready out front."

Jessica spent the next minutes trying to hide her messy look, covering up the dark bags under her eyes with makeup. She looked like she'd just gotten off a double in food service as she headed outside, yawning continually. She opened the car's door and sat in the back with her brother. The driver started the engine and drove off.

They stopped at an old, grey building with stained windows in Upper Manhattan. The structure resembled a haunted house and the only color was a large billboard hanging above the entrance reading "Jude Haul-Life Insurance". The siblings stepped outside as the driver waited in a parking lot nearby.

"This is where the man works?" Jessica said, surprised.

"I know, right?"

"I wouldn't trust him."

"Remember, I'm here to watch and make sure everything goes as planned."

"Yeah, whatever." She said rolling her eyes.

"Don't whatever me, Jessica. You can't screw things up…"

"Again. Say it, Giovanni."

"I wouldn't say that."

"You're just like father, you know that, right?"

"Hey! Knock it off. We're on the same side. I didn't want to come, alright?" Giovanni was talking while Jessica was already heading inside, determined to accomplish her mission. She walked in as if she owned the building and Giovanni followed her, both impressed and annoyed.

They got on the elevator and Giovanni pushed the button to the third floor.

"Now remember. This man owes us, which means we own him."

Jessica groaned. She kept looking straight ahead, tapping her foot. The doors opened, unveiling an old, dusty office. Jessica went to the secretary's desk, a fake smile plastered on her face, as she put her sunglasses back inside her handbag.

"Good morning."

"Good morning."

"I'm here to see Mister Haul. Is he in?"

"Yes, Miss. I'll be with you shortly"

"Oh, please don't call me, Miss. We're around the same age."

"Okay, my dear. Do you have an appointment, your name is—?" Jessica rolled her eyes.

" Jessica Lombardi and no, I don't need one."

"Lombardi, you said?"

"That's right."

"Let me see if he's free at the moment."

The secretary got up and Jessica turned towards Giovanni with a smirk. Her brother wasn't there as the elevator they left was heading to the ground floor. Perhaps, he believed in her after all. Jessica turned back towards Mister Haul's office door down the hall, over-hearing his conversation with his secretary. Then there were lapses in silence and the noise of a door opening from another room surprised Jessica. She quickly went down the hall and found his secretary standing in the middle of a messy office, but Jude Haul wasn't there. A gust of wind brought down a stack of papers on a desk, creating a bigger mess.

"Where is he?"

"I'm sorry, Lombardi but Mister Haul just left."

Jessica wanted to scream. That trick by the secretary had fooled her. She ran to the elevators, hoping to catch Haul and pressed the button furiously until it arrived. She was full of rage as her breathing had sped up. How could she let that guy slip away that easily? And where was Giovanni? Hating to admit, she could use his help right now. The elevator reached the ground floor and Jessica got out, looking to the left and right. She didn't see him but there was a back entrance that caught her attention. She ran for other entrance and as she passed by a service elevator, it opened revealing a sweating, panicked Jude Haul. She was ready to confront the weasel, but to her surprise,

Giovanni reached him first, with his gun drawn, pointing at Haul's head as he stepped off the elevator.

The man swallowed hard, and after a beat, began begging for his life between sobs. Jessica couldn't understand the words coming from his mouth..

"Giovanni?"

"It's ok, little one. I got this." Jessica hated that he diminished her in front of Jude Haul.

"I thought you were here to look on."

"Well, sometimes you have to catch the fish out of water."

"You could have said something."

"It's ok. I got this fine gentleman here to agree to our terms."

"Terms?"

"Yes, to give us a nice share of his business."

"I thought we were here to take the money."

"Please Miss, don't kill me." Haul said, interrupting their intense discussion.

"Speak to my sister again and I will." Giovanni spat at him, with a glare. Jessica ignored Haul and continued talking.

"That was the plan all along, wasn't it?"

"What do you mean, sister?"

"Have me scare him away while you catch him leaving."

"It was our father's idea. Do you like it?"

"You're just like him." She said, crossing her arms.

"Hey, I'm on your side."

"Yeah, yeah, screw you, Giovanni."

"Don't talk to your big brother like that."

"I'm done with the games."

Jessica turned her back, as her brother was still pointing his gun at Haul. She stormed out as her brother's faint call of her name echoed along with Haul's sobbing. Jessica pushed open the front glass door, so hard, she almost moved it out of its place. She started walking in the opposite direction from where the car was parked, elbowing people in her way. Jessica didn't know where she was heading as her mind was clouded with rage. She was angry and didn't expect that from her father. She had expected him to trust her, but clearly, she wasn't even capable of managing her expectations, much less, completing the task. She didn't care anymore. If Giovanni wanted to take matters into his own hands, she'd let him.

* * *

Jessica kept walking, somewhat lost, in the middle of downtown Manhattan. She rarely visited the place, but something about the spectacle was familiar. She kept walking until she reached Castello di Vino. To Jessica's delight, it was a comforting moment, remembering the day with Francesco here. She stood outside the pub, staring at the wooden sign as if time had stopped.

Lost in thought, Jessica stared at the sign, until the door opened and Federico came out to smoke.

"Signorina Jessica, what a pleasant surprise!"

"Ciao, Federico."

"Why are you standing here?" Federico asked confused.

"I'm not sure."

"Vieni, we are open!" Federico said after throwing out his cigarette and heading inside. Jessica hesitated for a moment before finally following him in. She took a seat at the bar.

"Gin, please. Double shot."

"Isn't it a bit early, signorina?"

"Is it your place?" she said, venom dripping from her words.

"As you wish." Federico said as he opened the bottle and poured her drink.

"Grazie."

"On the house."

Jessica spent a few minutes, glancing at her glass. She kept fiddling with it like a little child, making a game out of it.

"It's not poisoned."

"Why would it be?" She said arching her brow. "Besides it's all poison anyways, right?"

"Why don't you drink, then?"

"I'm just thinking."

"Rough day so far, signorina?"

"Rough is an understatement."

"Are you here for Francesco? He said he'll come by today."

Jessica's eyes widened and her heart skipped a beat.

"Is he really?" Jessica asked trying not to sound too pleased.

"Si, he has some business nearby," replied Federico, drying a wine glass with a towel. Jessica took a sip as she kept playing with the glass.

"If I may."

"Hmm?"

"You look like a mess, signorina."

"Tell me about it."

"You looked happier days ago."

"I have a sleeping problem."

"No, no. Not just tired."

"You can tell?" She said, setting the glass down with a sigh.

"I see many people here every day."

"Do they all look the same?"

" They don't all look the same, but I can tell how they feel. It's in the eyes. The eyes always give you away." Fredrico said with a wink.

Jessica wore a sad but sincere look as she took another sip— a bigger one this time.

"You work for the Giulianis, don't you?"

"I may or may not."

"I see."

"Is that a problema?"

"No, no."

"Why ask, then?"

"I was just wondering."

"But you work for the Lombardis."

"In a way."

"You are nice for a Lombardi," Federico said smiling. "I'm sure if the others in your family were as personable as yourself, New York would be very different."

Jessica smiled through another sip. She gathered that he was an optimist by nature and his genuine smile somehow both comforted and bothered Jessica. Despite this, she couldn't deny that she felt safe in his pub. It was refuge from her family business and from her own problems. Spirits lifted slightly by Federico's mood and her own spirits, Jessica kept up the friendly conversation and ordered two more doubles. She didn't know if she was drinking to pass time, or just to forget everything that had happened since she arrived back from Italy. It didn't matter now. She was enjoying this peace, and she savored her quiet buzz until the sound of the door creaking open brought her back to her senses.

12

AN UNEXPECTED MEETING

Lombardi and Giuliani Family

Jessica turned toward the door, watching Francesco enter, with the same look he had when they were with Elias.

"Ciao, Federico!" he shouted as he headed for the bar.

"Ciao, Francesco," Jessica said softly as he approached.

Francesco's eyes widened once he saw Jessica sitting at the bar. He looked quickly at Federico who was shrugging and then looked back to the Lombardi girl. She was sitting in the same spot they'd sat last time.

"Hey."

"You didn't expect to see me here again?"

"I didn't."

"Well. Surprise!" She chuckled softly.

"What are you doing here?"

"Drinking."

"Quite a bit, I must say," Federico interrupted as he served Francesco.

Jessica rolled her eyes.

"Here's to free drinks, and chance meetings." Francesco grinned and grabbed his glass raising it towards Jessica. She raised an empty one. Federico came quickly to fill hers and then returned to cleaning off the bar's counter. Francesco and Jessica toasted and took sips simultaneously.

"You look great."

"You're lying."

"Why?"

"Federico said I look like a mess." Francesco considered this.

"You don't to me."

"Then maybe it's the alcohol."

"Fredrico says you've had quite a bit to drink."

"I might have had a stormy day. We all do, don't we?"

Francesco nodded, agreeing. "So, what happened?"

Jessica took her time before answering. She took a long sip while staring at Federico still cleaning. Then, she fixed her hair letting it loose. Slowly, she turned and looked at the Giuliani. He was dressed in white, but the irony was not lost on her. He was far from innocent. His athletic body was facing hers, his knees touching her own. Francesco loosened his tie and took another sip. The two of them were thinking the same thing. Their families were the city's deadliest rivals and the smallest detail could be used against one other. Yet, both had other things in mind. Jessica cleared her throat.

"My business meeting went wrong today." She said, her eyes were glued to the floor.

"Just like the one with Elias?" Francesco chuckled, chiding her. Jessica glared at him, angry at his cockiness.

"You know what? I think I'll take my drink to go."

"What?"

"This was a bad idea coming here."

"Come on, I was kidding."

"No, you weren't."

"I didn't mean to hurt you."

"You didn't mean to?"

"Your acting as if I did."

"Stop trying me, Francesco."

The pub became silent as tensions grew. Only the towel scrubbing against the counter was echoing. Federico lifted his eyes, watching Jessica and Francesco glaring at each other.

"Umm, I should probably check the inventory. Torn tra un secondo." Federico said to himself, heading to the cellar in the back.

"Is he always like that?"

"Like what?"

"So pleasant."

"Actually, yes."

"How does he manage?"

"He made peace with what life throws at him."

"Wish I could do the same."

"I understand you." Francesco said, resting his hand on her shoulder.

"No, you don't," she said shrugging him off and taking another sip.

"What in your perfect life can possibly be so bad?"

"Perfect?" He scoffed. "Our families have been fighting for years, and it's only getting worse. And what's more? We don't have a place in the feud anyway." He said. He cursed himself for oversharing but decided he Jessica was harmless.

"You may understand me after all."

"I told you I did. So, what frustrates you, my dear?"

"I'll tell you if you promise not to talk about Elias again. If you bring him up again, I'll stab you between the eyes."

"No Elias jokes, I promise. "he said raising his hands in innocence. Maybe she wasn't so harmless after all.

"My brother, Giovanni used me as a diversion to get a job done today—a job that I was supposed to do alone."

"Why?"

"It was our father's idea. Neither of them believe in me."

"You were a little out of your woods when we first met," Francesco said, rubbing his neck. Jessica gave him a menacing glare, but it softened into sadness quickly.

"You're right. You, my brother, our fathers all make it seem so easy."

"Well, it isn't."

"How do you manage?"

"Sometimes, I don't but I keep pushing forward. My family needs me."

Jessica finished her gin in one big gulp and wiped off her lips.

"Mine doesn't."

"That's ridiculous."

"They don't believe in me, Francesco."

"I'm sure you're an excellent attorney."

"I don't want to be just a lawyer. I want to help."

"This business is not for everyone."

"I'm sure it's something you can master."

"It's something you grow into. Something that transforms you in order to fit in."

"Can you teach me?" Jessica gasped. The words that came out of her mouth she realized how crazy they were. She grabbed her forehead and Francesco chuckled. Jessica was serious. Francesco cleared his throat and took a deep breath.

"What do you mean, teach you?"

"Pretend I never said that. It's ridiculous. I didn't mean it.."

"I could, but that would hurt me and my family in the long run."

"What do you mean?"

"You shouldn't get involved in this career."

"Why not?"

"It changes you in ways you couldn't imagine."

"Did it change you?"

"Yes. I have to live with my sins each day."

"If you can live with the family business, then I can, too."

"Stay away from this, Jessica."

"Why?"

"You started a good life on the outside; don't ruin it."

"Why do you care so much, ?" Jessica stared into Francesco's eyes which betrayed her lack of anger. There was something else pooling inside them and Francesco knew what it was. Jessica didn't want to argue knowing Francesco was right. A minute passed with no conversation, but it felt like hours. Jessica sighed and the tension eased up a little. She wanted to stop this conversation and talk about something else instead. Her cheeks were warming from the gin and her palms were sweating so she wiped them on her pants. She felt lightly buzzed, but far from drunk, and couldn't tell if the warm feeling coursing through her veins was the fault of the liquor, or the man sitting beside her.

She looked up at him only to find he'd been staring at her. He wasn't simply watching her anymore, and his eyes contained something she was sure hers did as well-desire. He leaned in close to hear ear and she could feel his breath on her neck as he spoke, which only made her feel hotter.

"Why do I care?" he said, in a low voice. She could feel his lips vibrating less than an inch from her neck.

She swallowed hard.

He gently cupped her chin in his hand and turned her head so her eyes met his.

"I think I know you better than anyone else."

She wanted to slap him for his forwardness, but her limbs felt like lead. She considered this for a moment. Maybe he really did understand her; they were practically in the same boat. Before she could react, he'd tilted her head and pressed his soft lips to hers. He pulled her into a long, smooth kiss that left them both winded when they finally pulled apart. Jessica stepped off the barstool, trying to put some distance between herself and Francesco.

"Where are you going?" Francesco said, his voice low and husky.

Jessica stepped back and cleared her throat. She couldn't look him in the eyes, but she felt a blush warming her cheeks.

"I should get going." Jessica lifted her bag and hastened to the front door. She dared a final glance over her shoulder as she pushed open the pub door. Francesco's eyes were glued to her, and she cursed herself for looking back. The sound of the door closing was the only thing that brought him back to his senses. Francesco emptied his glass, staring at the closed door.

"You can come out now." Francesco said, wiping a hand down his face, with a sigh. He leaned over the bar to grab the half-empty bottle of wine, pouring himself drink.

"So…"

"Federico, please."

"You followed, Consigli."

"I didn't."

"I saw otherwise."

"Don't you have anything better to do?"

"The place is empty."

"So, you don't. "He said shaking his head and taking another sip.

"Was it good?"

"Sta'zitto Federico."

"Don't tell me to shut up, Francesco."

"Why were you watching?"

"I wasn't."

"It doesn't seem that way."

"I was coming back when I saw the look on your eyes."

"What look?"

"Dai Federico. Don't hide from zio."

"You're no zio, Federico."

"I'll soon be."

"Jessica's right. Why are you always like that?"

"Jessica's right huh? Like what?"

"So happy."

"I'm happy for my amico."

"There's nothing to be happy about." he scoffed. "We're living in New York."

"There are plenty of reasons to be happy."

"She's a Lombardi."

"A Lombardi that kissed you, Francesco! Svegliati! The girl likes you."

"She does."

"And you like her."

Francesco knew Federico was right. He liked the Lombardi girl and he enjoyed that kiss, more than he wanted to admit. Francesco finished his drink, pouring himself another.

"It's a little too early to get drunk."

"Something keeps bugging me."

"It's called amore."

Francesco sighed. "What should I do?"

"Seguine il tuo cuore"

"Don't give me that 'follow your heart' shit, Federico."

Federico shrugged as he tidied up the glasses on the shelves behind him. Francesco drank as the first rain-drops outside pattered the roof and windows, like rocks on glass. Francesco kept going, thinking about that kiss; that perfect, soft, Lombardi kiss. He'd had lovers but this was a new feeling one that began to consume him. It only made him want more of that Lombardi girl.

Francesco spent the rest of his morning sitting there, sipping his wine, as the customers poured in from the rain.

* * *

Meanwhile, Jessica was walking home, more confused and

lost than when she first arrived from Italy. The raindrops sprinkled down her face but she didn't feel them. She still felt hot but she couldn't tell if it was because of the liquor or her kiss with Francesco. *Probably both.* The sound of traffic and people trying to escape the rain muffled her thoughts. She crossed a few streets without noticing the cars coming towards her. What came over Jessica Lombardi? Why did she do such a forbidden thing? How could she betray her family as she did? Part of her berated herself for being so careless. She knew better than to go drinking during the day, and she'd known it was foolish to go back to Castello di Vino. Another part of her didn't want to admit that she'd enjoyed every second of it and craved more. She bit her lip still feeling the sting of Francesco's mouth on hers. She replayed the kiss over and over in her mind. The logical side of her brain snapped her back to reality. She realized Francesco probably thought she was an easy conquest. She felt rage boiling up inside of her as the thought of him being so cocky. She shook her head as she continued down the rain-slicked street. She decided it was best to stay on her side of the city. One wrong move and everything would come crashing down around them. It was dangerous to get involved with Francesco, and they both knew it. Jessica chalked it up to a foolish, yet happy accident.

13

THE FUNERAL

The FBI

The rain was getting heavier, with the drops landing on the windows of the 5th Precinct like small bombs, trying to push their way inside. Agent Thomas Miller watched the rain trickle down the window panes. The way the rain moved was soothing. An occasional thunder would cause the old windows to rattle and the room's lights flicker. It was a lousy day for anyone who wanted to go for a walk, and it only added to the gloom settling over the NYPD.

Thomas filled his glass with whiskey and lit his cigarette. It felt like a day off. His glass was half full and its ice cubes melted causing his glass to mimic the wet windows outside. His cigarette's ashes fell on the ground slowly burning away while Thomas let his mind take him elsewhere. He dropped what remained of the cigarette on the ground, stomping out the aches. Thomas then scratched the scruffy beard that he hadn't shaved in days. The bags under his eyes made him look twenty years older. He kept contemplating the scene of Jonathan's dead body in the holding cell. If he could remove it from his subconscious, he would but the thought kept resurfacing, giving him nightmares. Thomas would wake up with a start, beaded in sweat and breathing heavily.

Thomas took out another cigarette and lit it up. He took a drag, blowing the smoke towards the windows. He was so occupied with the raindrops and the thought of Jonathan, he didn't realize for the past few seconds, Garcia had been hovering behind him.

"Umm, sir?" Garcia said, clearing her throat.

"Hmm?"

"It's time, sir."

"For?"

"The funeral."

"Jonathan?"

"Yes, sir. Jonathan and Terry."

"Okay."

"Are you not coming?"

"Why should I?"

"You're the lead investigator, sir. You gave a wonderful speech. The captain believes you should go."

"I killed that man."

"Sir, if I may…"

"You may not."

"You didn't kill him, sir. You did what any officer of integrity would think is right."

"So, did the families?"

"You're not the same, sir!"

"Hmm."

Garcia watched as Thomas took another cigarette out, taking a drag and leaving the pack on the desk. He didn't turn around to talk to Garcia while they were talking.

"Sir, I can't bear to see you like this."

"Get used to it."

"Well, I can't."

Agent Garcia sighed. "Do you want their deaths to be in vain?" Garcia now began to raise her voice. "Is this the first death you've encountered, sir?" Thomas remained silent. "You want me to go on with the clichés? Ok, fine then. Is that what Terry wanted? You're holed up in your shithole office, whining about what? Terry wanted to do the right thing in the end, and he trusted you. Now, you're going to let him and his family down. If you don't come, sir, be ready to receive my resignation." Garcia stormed out, slamming the door behind.

Thomas was smiling, still following the raindrops which began to form these little weird-shaped rivers on the window sill.

I taught you well, Garcia. he thought to himself as he took another long drag, Garcia was right, but he couldn't bring himself to go -not yet.

For the next twenty minutes, Agent Miller enjoyed

himself —drinking and smoking, glass after glass, drag after drag, until his brain was numb enough for him to step out. He was ready to face the police officers who were the remaining good apples on the force.

Thomas could hardly walk a straight line but still decided to go to the funeral. He didn't say a word to Garcia; he let the rain wash away his guilt and pain. The rain was coming down hard across his face; his jaw resembled a waterfall. His clothes were drenched to an entirely new shade, making it troublesome to walk ahead, but it was freeing. Thomas Miller was feeling dizzy, as everything around him was spinning, but he kept walking. The officers, city workers, families, and community members were scrambling, trying to find a place, away from the heavy rain. Still, Agent Miller was taking long, slow strides.

Each step he took, he thought of Jonathan. Each time Thomas tripped, he thought of the "homeless" man in the cell for some odd reason. He screwed up but he had to deal with the mess. Miller covered his face to avoid the water entering his tired, red eyes. For a long twenty minutes, Thomas started to sing an old song about a man killed in the war. He was singing off the top of his lungs, but the rain and thunder muffled his hoarse voice. Agent Miller kept on singing until he reached the cemetery.

An ocean of black umbrellas covered the sight of the surrounding graves. Thomas wanted to sit in the back and watch from afar but knew that would be disrespectful. He walked into the crowd as if he had lost a family member, taking his time with each step. He pushed his way through the crowd of officers dressed appropriately for the fallen officers. Thomas was the only one in a trench coat, its beige color was soaked almost into brown. He made his way to the front row; the two coffins were draped in two American flags. He looked around seeing the Mayor, Police Commissioner, City Council and others of high ranking in the city. The agent shook hands and then noticed an old woman sobbing, Jonathan's name. The captain of the 7th Precinct stood respectfully, waiting for the procession to begin. Agent Garcia was next to the captain. She faintly smiled at Thomas before turning her attention to the procession.

The silence overtook the loud sounds of rain, to Thomas' ears, but then was interrupted by the constant yelling of the old woman. Thomas was pale and felt the urge of vomiting, but he remained still. The wails faded when a young pastor came up and stood between the two coffins.

"Brother and sisters, hope doesn't disappoint, because the love of God has been poured out into our hearts." Thomas Miller used to ridicule the people of God, but on this day, he stood respectfully, listening. The pastor spoke for a few minutes and it was time for the captain to say a few words. The pastor prayed in silence before the captain took position.

"We lost two exemplary men this week. Their morals and dedication to the force will be missed by all, especially the people who had worked with them. For the past few days, the 5th precinct appears darker without their presence." He took a long pause before taking a deep breath. His eyes met Thomas'. "Many accused them of being bribed, compromised and undutiful. Many tried to hurt them, but they were always ready when the call came in. But now that we need these two officers the most, they're not with us and they will be truly missed. Mrs. Howards… my sincerest condolences and apologies." The captain returned to the mourning crowd and stood next to Garcia.

Silence draped over the next few minutes as the sound of the rain overtook the burial. Mourners wished their farewells to the fallen officers one by one passing by the caskets and placing flowers on them. Then, as the diggers began their task, the crowd of mourners slowly began dispersing; most towards the old woman, Terry's mother, to pay their respects. Thomas went to the captain.

"Touching speech, Captain! It's a shame you don't believe any of it."

"What did you expect me to say?"

"The truth."

"Here? In front of Jonathan's mother?"

"The old woman thinks he's a hero."

"But he is."

"No. He is a fucking victim."

"Bold statement, coming from an outsider."

"What are you implying?"

"You're the one who placed him in that cell."

Thomas scoffed. "Goodbye, Captain."

Thomas made his way through the cemetery along with the remaining mob. When he got closer to Garcia's car, he leaned, under an evergreen, shielding himself from the rain as he lit a cigarette. The cold weather took away his brief moments of grief as did the Captain's words. He would take him down along with the families and every corrupt officer in the precinct.

Thomas was on his second cigarette when Garcia emerged heading in his direction.

"Glad you came to your senses, sir." Garcia unlocked the doors and quickly climbed into the car.

"Glad you encouraged me." Thomas shook his wet hair and wadded up his drenched coat, tossing it into the floorboard. Garcia looked at him strangely.

"What's the plan, sir?"

"We'll take them down."

"The families, you mean?"

"The families, the fucking captain, and every last one of those damn corrupt officers in the 7th. Every last fucking one."

"Sir, we have no leads."

"We don't yet but we'll find something."

"How?"

"I have agents on this back in Quantico. However, I want you to gather information on every single shop bought out by the Italians. Check everywhere that money can be made, even the restaurants and wine shops. I want to know exactly how much of New York is under their thumbs."

"Are we going door knocking?"

"Kind of."

"Ok, sir. I'll get right on it."

"Thank you, Garcia."

Garcia smiled and started the car. The car's heater warmed them both. Thomas Miller closed his eyes welcoming the warmness. Before long, he was asleep. The man had to rest, as the next coming days would be the hardest for the NYPD.

14

A NIGHT OUT AT CASTELLO

The Lombardi and Giuliani Families

Francesco had spent the week, helping out his mother and father, to remodel the mansion . In between, he'd spend his nights running the usual family business operations. After resting, he'd start his days off moving boxes and tidying up his space. His father, Luca and little brother were ready to paint the house together. Every few years, the Giulianis did this as a family and it was something that brought them closer. Though Francesco's mind was on the remodeling, he was thinking more about the Lombardi girl. It made him feel guilty, but he had enjoyed that kiss. He was lucky to see her in Castello and didn't know when he'd meet her again. That anticipation tugged at him. He wanted to meet Jessica again.

Francesco was almost finished packing his stuff. He

took a break to sit in the middle of his room, encircled by the large boxes. Holding an old family album on his lap, he browsed through the photos, most with his brother and cousins. They used to have fun before Francesco started working for the family. He continued surveying the old stuff in his bedroom when he came across an aged agenda with a golden monogram of the letter 'L' on it. It was Luca's. Francesco opened it flipping the pages like he was reading a magazine. As he flipped, he realized this was a business plan. He paused. A smile he couldn't hold back crept up his face. He continued flipping until he reached the letter L —'Lombardi Mansion House Phone' right under 'Luca's Office Phone number'.

Francesco got up and headed to the nearest phone booth. He spent a few minutes staring at the phone and looking over the number. *It couldn't be this easy, right?* Why did his father have the Lombardi number stashed away in his agenda? His hands were shaking and his palms were getting sweaty. He wiped them on his pants and picked up the phone resembling one expecting bad news from his doctor. Francesco took a deep breath and dialed. With each ring, his heart raced.

"Pronto?" It was the voice of an old woman.

"Ciao. Is Jessica there?" Francesco said changing his voice.

"Un attimo."

Seconds later, he heard the voice that made his heart jump. "Hello?"

"Hi Jessica. It's Francesco."

Jessica smiled hearing his voice and when he said his name her heart did a little flip-flop in her chest.

"H—hi. Where did you get my number?" She said, twirling a lock of her hair.

"An old program in the office."

"Well, I'm glad you called."

"Do you want to meet, at our usual place?"

"Our *usual place*?" Jessica said with a smirk. Francesco could hear it in her voice.

"You know, Castello." He said with a chuckle.

"Today?"

"Tonight."

"Oh! Yes. 9 PM?"

"I'll be waiting."

"I'll be there."

Francesco hung up, memorizing the Lombardi Mansion phone number before tossing the agenda in a nearby dumpster. It was already 5 PM. He rushed home to his bathroom, to get ready although it will be in four hours.

Jessica hung up, feeling giddy, like the caller told her she'd landed a new job. Her grandmother was eavesdropping the whole time.

"Nipotina, who was that?"

"Nothing, nothing."

"What is at 9?"

"I have an arrangement."

"A date? With who?"

"Not a date. An arrangement."

"You're trying to fool me? Look yourself in the mirror."

"What?"

"You smile like you won all the money in the world."

"I don't." Jessica lied, trying to hide her smile but she couldn't.

"Shame on you for not trusting your nonna."

"We'll talk later, I promise. I have to go now." Jessica ran up to her room, locking the door. She laid her clothes out on her bed, trying to decide what to wear. A red summer dress, with black heels, and a red leather bag seemed appropriate. Jessica took a shower and then put on her makeup and styled her hair.

Francesco told his driver, Geno to take him to Castello di Vino, as Jessica called a cab from her room.

It was almost 9 and Francesco had arrived early already moving into his second glass of wine. A few days back, the place was empty and now it was packed. Traditional Italian music was playing that blended perfectly with voices inside the pub. The lights from the old chandeliers and the candles on each table offered a soothing ambiance. Everyone was enjoying themselves, except Francesco who was uptight. Federico was busy serving but noticed Francesco's face from afar. "It'll be fine. You'll do okay," Federico said serving Francesco another glass of wine. Francesco looked at his friend and smiled.

* * *

Francesco had just finished his drink when the pub door opened, the bells overhead chiming quietly amidst the evening company banter. He turned to see Jessica stepping inside, the cool night wind ruffling her red dress and hair. She scanned the room for a moment until her eyes met Francesco's and she waved. He smiled at her and motioned for her to join him at the

bar. "I'd figure you'd wear another one of your white suits." Jessica said, tugging on the sleeve of his black suit.

"What's wrong with this?"

"Nothing. You look great! But tonight, you've changed."

Jessica's smile rivaled Francesco's. His own smile had hooked her, and his eyes were luring her in. She found it hard to look away, but eventually she did, turning to Fredrico

instead. "May I have a gin, please."

"I was thinking maybe we should go somewhere else tonight." Francesco said, pulling her back in.

"You've been drinking already, and I like it here." She said, keeping her gaze on Fredrico who was diligently preparing her drink.

"Fine." Francesco said, lifting a hand to her face, and cupping her chin, softly. He turned her to face him, but she playfully batted his hand away.

"Next time, take me to dinner." Jessica winked while picking up her glass. Federico had already filled

Francesco's glass again. Jessica raised hers with a nod to Francesco.

"To happy accidents," she said.

Francesco raised his. "To happy coincidences."

They both took a sip.

"So how's business, Jessica?"

"We're not here to talk about business."

"Okay."

"Tell me about you and your family."

"Like you don't know about them?"

"I'm kidding. You mean in Italy. "No."

"Well, I have a younger brother, Giovanni."

"Yes, I know him."

"Really? How?"

"No business talks, remember."

"So, what is your brother like?"

"Lately, he's been behaving strangely."

"Strangely how?"

"He always seems angry."

"Angry with you?"

"He says I'm not around enough."

"That's what you meant the other day."

"You mean about the family business, I see?"

"Yes. It changes the people around you."

"Exactly."

"I understand what you're going through."

"Tell me about our mother, Italy. I haven't been there since I was a boy."

"You know. It's beautiful. The best coffee and vino.

But I like it in America better. Too many small streets there."

"Why did you chose law?"

"I wanted to help my family business."

"Shady lawyer?"

"Something like that but I would only be in what's legal."

"You'll find a way to get into the gray areas though."

"Unfortunately, yes which does me no good."

"Because of Michael, Yes?"

"No. I'm the one everyone relies on and it's exhausting."

"Sometimes you have to step back."

Jessica looked naughty while smiling and taking a sip. Francesco was drawn in and didn't notice anyone else except the two of them. It was if they were in a bubble, blocking out everything. Every time they paused, he couldn't stop thinking how stunning Jessica looked.

Jessica's heart was racing.

It made her wet inside but she held her poise.

The night went on as they chatted for hours, like two friends who reunited after many years. The pub was nearly empty and the two of them were still sitting at the bar. The two mobster rivals had more in common than they could imagine. Francesco loved jazz and Jessica used to be in a jazz band as the lead singer. They had a passion for beaches, reading, and backgammon, a game neither of them had played in ages.

Castello di Vino was now empty and Jessica with

Francesco were still talking, laughing, and touching. Her hands were rubbing Francesco's legs as his hands were traveling up and down her arm. They were close and their bodies almost met.

"I hate to break up your party but Castello is closing for tonight" Federico shouted from the back.

"It was fun tonight," said Francesco.

"It really was. I'm glad you called."

"I want to meet you again. Did you have a good time?"

"I did."

"Lunch tomorrow?"

"Ok."

"Let's start here and find a nice place."

"At 3?"

"Sounds good." Francesco stood up, escorting Jessica out. He lifted his arm hailing a taxi which screeched to a stop in front of them.

"This is goodnight, then." he breathed, holding Jessica close. She didn't answer but leaned in for a kiss— a long one, sliding her tongue up and down inside Francesco's mouth. Then she stepped back, smiling.

"No, this is my goodnight." Jessica got in the cab and left.

Francesco waited on the dark road, watching as she vanished into the night, nothing but an intoxicating memory and a fading tingle on his lips.

15

A DARK SECRET

Lombardi Family

It was late —way past the time anyone in the Lombardi household stayed awake. Jessica pulled out the keys from her purse and opened the door, trying not to wake those sleeping inside. She took off her heels and headed to her room, creeping like a burglar. Once up the stairs, she heard something and almost dropped the heels and purse. She turned around, seeing her grandmother at the base of the stairs. The old woman nodded and came up, following the young girl to her room. Jessica sat on the bed, smiling and kicking her feet back and forth.

"Arrangement, huh?" her grandmother said in a thick Italian accent.

"Yes, grandma, I told you I had an arrangement."

"Dai, don't lie to your nonna. Where were you?" She

asked the question, but she was smiling through her wrinkles. It had been some time since she last seen her granddaughter so happy.

"At Castello di Vino. Do you know it?"

The older woman frowned. "The Giuliani pub?"

"Yes?" Jessica said, furrowing her brow.

"It's one of the Giulianis' hangouts. They have many back in Italy."

"Really, grandma?"

"Si."

"I didn't know it was *theirs*.." Jessica poured extra animosity into the last word, but deep down, she didn't mean it. She'd come to know one of the Giulianis tonight, and if the rest of the family was anything like them, they might be worth getting to know as well.

"What were you doing there?" Her grandmother's words snapped her back from her thoughts.

Still smiling, she couldn't look at her grandmother. "I went to meet someone" she whispered, hiding her face like a little girl who'd done something bad.

Her grandmother's eyes widened. "Lo sapevo!" her grandmother blurted. "Who is it? Some Giuliani guy?"

Jessica stood up, wandering around the room for a moment, pacing back and forth until finally returning to the bed.

She wasn't she what more she should divulge, but her grandmothers interest seemed genuine, and she felt like she could trust

her. "You could say that."

Her grandmother paused, absorbing her response. Jessica felt doubt set in—maybe she shouldn't have told her nonna after all.

"Nipotina. Is he good-looking?"

"Nonna!"

"What? If he is not handsome, then he must have lots of money. Those are the only two attractive qualities for a Giuliani man."

"Stop joking, grandma."

"Who is it?"

"His name's Francesco Giuliani."

"Oh, I don't know the Ragazzo. I only know Luca."

"His father?"

"Si, my husband and I did a lot of business with his family before the war."

"Ok."

"Did you have fun? You can't hide your happiness."

"It was great, grandma. Tomorrow we are meeting for lunch."

"A true principe. What a gentleman. Oooh, I can't wait to tell the others."

"Grandma, no. Please."

"Why?"

"I don't want father or Giovanni to kill me for dating a Giuliani."

"They won't!"

"They will. They're in the business and so is Francesco, these old timers can't think straight."

"This will be our little secret, then?"

"Yes, for now. I'm afraid."

"I won't tell."

"You promise?"

"Of course, Nipotina. Of course." Jessica was surprised her grandmother was being so open-minded. Part of her knew her grandmother valued love over war, but another part of her expected the be disowned after sharing her news.

Jessica rushed for a hug almost dropping her grandmother from the bed. As she did, she felt relieved.

"Go to sleep, Nipotina. Tomorrow, you have a big lunch." Her grandmother winked leaving the room. Jessica took off her clothes and lied down. She didn't know if it was the gin or Francesco, but everything was spinning so sweetly. She closed her eyes and within minutes, she was sound asleep.

16

SINS OF THE SON

Lombardi, Giuliani and Saltinotti Family

Francesco opened his eyes and it was still dark out. He turned over and check his clock; it read 6:07 a.m. He had to get up and slowly rose; spending a few minutes, trying to clear his head.

It's been two weeks since the first dinner date with Jessica. Since then, they've met almost daily, often taking long walks near the harbor and drinking at night at Castello di Vino. Francesco felt different and was happy to be away having fun. Finally, he'd found something worthwhile to take his mind off the family business. Despite the immense joy he had from his secret meetings with Jessica, the pressure he had from making sure there were no fuck-ups weighed down on his shoulders. He got up and put on his white suit. He had a date with Jessica again tonight and wanted to finish up his errands early as possible.

Francesco headed down to the dining room, finding his father was already awake at the head of the table. The aroma of freshly brewed espresso mixed with the smell of boiled eggs filled its air. Luca was reading the newspaper when Francesco entered. He kissed his father on the cheeks and took a seat.

"Good morning, Francesco."

"Good morning, father. How was your sleep?"

"Very good and you?"

"Eccellente! Why are you up so early?"

"I wanted to see you before you go."

"I'm not leaving for another two hours, papa."

"Still. I want to make sure you are prepared."

"What is going on?."

"We can't have another killing associated with our family name."

"I'm not going to do a cleaning job today."

"I'm afraid it may turn out that way."

"What do you mean?"

"You don't know where the Saltinottis' loyalty lies."

"So?"

"It's your job going to find out why they left our alliance and see if we can do something to win them back."

"That bastard Andrea stopped being loyal. Fuck him, papa."

"Francesco, calmati. I don't want to see another assassination."

"But those rats—"

"No, my son. We're making mistakes and must take another approach. We can't keep killing everyone who decides to leave our accord. Do you understand?"

"Yes, father. I'll do my best."

"Also, there's something else. I heard that an old schoolmate of yours will be there."

"Hmm—who?"

"Giovanni Lombardi."

"What?"

"Yes, he and a few of those Lombardis are trying to convince the Saltinottis to expand business with them. I believe he will be there at nine and so will you."

"I'll be there before him, then."

"I'd do it myself Francesco, but I am getting too old."

"I know father, it's okay. You've prepared me well."

"The family's harbor business is on your shoulders now. I trust you to honor our name."

"Thank you." Francesco replied, grabbing an apple from the dish at the middle of the table.

Francesco went back to his room to prepare for one of the biggest days of his career. Winning over a family that decided to part ways was a tall task. And yet, there was another act of betrayal; the third in less than two months. The Giulianis were losing their grip and it was evident from Davide's Baldinotti's last words that still echoed in Francesco's mind. He had to do something. His father was close to retiring and Francesco wasn't as good as his father in regards to negotiating. The young man had a quick temper and the trigger was his way out.

* * *

It was almost nine and Francesco had pulled off. Watching his family's mansion , he remembered why the Giulianis were so powerful. Their loyalty was prized, more than any other family's loyalty despite the recent letdowns. When they got into the union business less than ten years ago, they were small petty players. Nowadays, they are the kings of drug trafficking, shipping guns, and real estate. The Giuliani harbor is where the family smuggled everything inside. With the Lombardis expanding its territory close to the harbor, it was affecting the Giulianis trafficking business which made them an expensive tax that the Saltinottis could no longer afford.

Francesco stopped at the gate decorated with two large *S* on each side. There were two guards outside, armed with their Thompson 28's. The Saltinotti's terrace surrounded the house like a miniature Central Park. There were evergreen trees and greenery which deco-rated the outside of the marble mansion . It'd been a while since Francesco had last visited and the elegant home of the Saltinotti's and it had always amazed him.

The guards watched Francesco and were instructed to expect anything. Francesco knew the mafia families heard about how Davide Baldinotti had been taken out.

The young heir was a hard-to-miss fellow, always dressed in a white suit and wide brim. Francesco confidently, but cautiously approached the guards, but stopped short when a whistle, from behind him, caught his attention. Francesco turned around seeing Giovanni Lombardi.

"Hello, Francesco."

"Giovanni!" Francesco feigned familiarity as he clapped Giovanni on the back.

"What are you doing here?"

"I'm here to talk to Andrea."

"I'm afraid you chose the wrong time, my friend."

"How come?" Giovanni said, making his way through the gated courtyard at the behest of the armed guards.

"Today, my family will make the deal of a lifetime with the Saltinottis."

"Oh, yeah. Then, I picked the perfect day to see you go with your hands empty." he chuckled, but there was no humor in his voice.

"This isn't a western comedy, Francesco."

"Why would it be?"

"Lately, the only thing you Giuliani's do is—?"

"I see you are mistaken."

Francesco balled his fists while his blood boiled. He knew Giovanni was somewhat right, but out of respect for Jessica, he kept his cool.

The two men proceeded through the double doors and were escorted to the big dining hall. There was a mural of 'Creation of Adam' which covered the ceiling.

When they came in, Andrea Saldinotti was already seated at the head of the table in the room's center.

The old don was wearing a black tuxedo, with a fedora hat which was carefully placed in front of him. His light mustache along with his thick eyebrows, made him look intimidating.

"I should have known you would show up, Francesco Giuliani. Have a seat— you too." Andrea summoned the maid, standing in the corner, with his hand.

"Gin for Giovanni and our finest wine for my *friend*, Francesco." Francesco and Giovanni took their places next to Andrea. Francesco frowned, but quickly assumed a neutral expression as he took his seat. The way Andrea called him his friend sent a chill up his spine. They weren't friends.

"Giovanni, I know why you are here. But you Francesco, are you here to kill me? I know what you did to our poor friend, Davide."

"No, Andrea, I'm here to see our little proposal is back on the table." Francesco chuckled, setting his hat on the table and loosening his tie, slightly. He tried to keep his composure, but the truth was, he was ready to leave the moment he'd stepped out of the Fiat.

"Ha, I see. So, Papa doesn't want you to kill anymore?"

For whatever reason, Andrea was being very direct, and somewhat hostile. Francesco assumed Andrea was behaving this way to shake him up, but he wasn't going to take the bait. He smiled, tracing a finger around the stitching in his wide brim, and said, "If it were up to me, you'd been dead a long time ago, Andrea but I have respect for made men."

"The boy has humor. You've clearly taken that from Sofia." Andrea skimmed his finger over his mustache. Andrea knew bringing up Francesco's mother was a low blow, but he was going to get a rise out of him, make him lose his temper. The maid broke the tension, bringing in a serving tray with the wine, gin, and glasses for the guests. She then hastily left after a rushed bow.

"Don't you talk about my mother." Francesco said, his voice low, eyes trained on the glossed, cherry oak tabletop.

"Oh, yes. La Famiglia e Tutto, my ass. You're bringing your deal back to the table. Go on, I will hear you *now*. "Andrea said, waving his hand. This wasn't how the negotiating was supposed to go. Andrea kept the ball in his court the whole time, and left Francesco on defense. He'd hoped he would be able to have an enjoyable conversation beforehand to butter up the old don, but Andrea wasn't having it. Besides, it was dangerous to openly negotiate with Giovanni around, but he'd have to make do with his wits and salvage their relationship somehow.

Francesco cleared his throat and sat up straighter. "We will lower the commission and fees for all your imports. We'll even offer you more protection than before. We have more manpower than the Lombardis."

"You, Giulianis are that desperate. Aren't you?"

"I'm here only to seal a deal. "Francesco said with a wink and sip of his wine.

"You see, Francesco. My lovely Lombardi comrades know who's running these streets." Andrea said, patting Giovanni on the back, almost a little too hard. "They offer me more of the harbor in exchange for lower fees. They don't rent like you, goddamn Giulianis."

Francesco sat stone-still, like a statue, dressed in white, red wine in hand. The Lombardis didn't want to simply strike a deal, they were here to bury the Giulianis once and for all. Francesco looked at Giovanni— he was smiling, enjoying his drink, savoring this.

"What do these fucking Lombardis get out of this? They're basically giving you this deal for nothing."

"Why do I care, Francesco? I get what I want, access to move my goods. I keep the piers that I already use and just pay a fair fee to my new partners, the Lombardis for new ones." The fact that he kept mentioning the Lombardi's as his friends and partners made Francesco's blood boil.

Francesco turned to Giovanni. If it was up to him, he would have killed both but his father told him no bloodshed. His father was right after all—once you take out all of the family heads, you have no one to deal with, a fact that was simultaneously an advantage and disadvantage. He could sway the existing bosses, but if new factions arose from the dust of the old families, a whole new war would be upon them. He had to keep his temper in check.

"That's a bullshit of a deal, Giovanni and you know it."

"We want you out of the picture, Francesco."

"Where's your honor?"

"Where was your honor when you killed Davide?"

"He broke the rules and betrayed us."

"This is not Italy, Francesco. Forget the old ways and change. We don't go around killing made men just because we feel like it." Giovanni slammed his glass on the table and Francesco glared back at him. His hand slid closer to his gun but didn't want to pull it out.

"I guess it's a done deal, then. May your partnership flourish. Gentlemen, if you'll excuse me." Francesco grabbed his hat and headed for the door. At the entrance, he said, "Remember Andrea. The old rules still apply. Ask Davide."

* * *

As Francesco drove off, his mind was cluttered. Not only did *he* lose, the Giulianis lost the harbor. His head was spinning because his family's business was falling apart, right under his feet. He stopped the car and decide to take walk back to the Saltinotti Mansion . There was one way to settle this. He hid behind a nearby dumpster and waited for nearly two hours. He saw Giovanni leave the mansion, smiling. He'd love to take that smirk off his face. They never really got along but there was one thing that would stop him. He thought of Jessica. He was her brother. He couldn't do that to her. Hurting her like that would kill him if not physically, then emotionally for the rest of his life. When Giovanni drove off, a black limo pulled up minutes later. Its tinted windows were reflecting off the sunlight. The big 'S' on its wheels made clear this was Andrea's. He would be out soon enough.

Andrea sauntered out towards the limo. The old don had won— he won the battle with the Giulianis and now the Lombardis were under him. This was the perfect power play. But that would cost the don his life. Andrea was alone, once his guards opened the double iron doors of the mansion . He didn't bother having his guards accompany him to the limo as they closed the doors.

The driver got out and rushed to open the door and bowed as Andrea made his way to the limo. Everyone feared Andrea except one man; the man in a white suit crossing the street, carrying his Colt M1911A1.

Seven bullets; that's all he had and needed. He aimed, pointing at the guard on the right. A loud gunshot echoed outside the Saltinotti mansion, activating the alarm of a black Sedan less than a block away. The guard fell to the ground and another drew his gun but it was too late. The bullet from the Colt pierced his scalp right between his eyes. He fell to the ground joining his comrade.

Andrea was frightened like an animal in the desert running for its life. Francesco fired another three consecutive gunshots; which pierced Andrea's heart, lung, and head. The impact of the gunshots thrust him forward and Andrea fell into the double iron doors, struggling to push them open, but slumped in the driveway, his blood gathering in a warm, sticky puddle around his body. The driver was all who remained. He raised his arms and kneeled pleading for his life. The sixth and final gunshot was the last thing heard. The bullet penetrated his forehead, splattering his brain on the pavement.

Francesco walked over to each of the four dead men. This execution was worse than Terry's and Davide. Francesco put his gun inside his suit jacket and started running.

17

THE WITNESS

The FBI

Agent Thomas Miller was sitting in his office, beneath heavy cloud of smoke and the smell of Vodka. His cigarette pack was nearly full despite it smelling like he'd chain-smoked all of them. The office windows were open, allowing a light breeze that made the papers on his desk fly around from time to time. He needed clean air for once. The sunlight filtered in through his window and onto his desk where piles of folders, towered like high-rises. Thomas documented everything that came to mind, passing notes to Garcia who was sitting on a couch a few feet away. The two had spent the past few weeks focusing on everything owned and rented by the Lombardi and Giuliani families. They made a list of family homes, businesses, and other properties under family members' names. There was no incriminating evidence yet, but they needed all the information they could get their hands on.

Before Miller took a break, he had just got finished with Francesco Giuliani's file which was thinner than a first grader's report card. The man known to the mafia world as the *Man in White* didn't even have a parking ticket. Thomas was about to move on to Jessica Lombardi's file when his phone rang. Garcia looked up from Giovanni's rap sheet, looking to Thomas for word on a breakthrough.

"Yep. That's me," he said. Then his expression quickly saddened, as if he just heard of the death of a relative. "What? Where? I'm on my way." he said hanging up the phone and grabbing his trench coat.

"Garcia, we've got to go, now. I think we've got a lead." He opened his office door and they headed quickly to the parking lot of the 5th precinct. Garcia didn't bother to ask what was happening. She hurried to try to catch up as Thomas was sprinting ahead.

Thomas told Garcia what he'd been told over the phone. He explained how Andrea Saltinotti had been shot along with two of his guards and his driver, out in front of his mansion. Once they arrived, they found the area blocked off by police, neighbors, and reporters desperately trying to cover what happened.

Thomas parked the black Tahoe and rushed towards the crime scene. He pushed Like Moses parting the red sea, Miller motioned for everyone to move out of the way, so he and Garcia could come through. The crowd spoke in whispers and the humming was interrupted by the sound of the cameras.

An officer of the 7th precinct said, "Clear the way, please." Agents Miller and Garcia passed the officer and went under the yellow tape surrounding the mansion .

"We're lucky the forensics team hasn't arrived yet."

"Lucky how, sir?"

"Those idiots might be working with the families."

"Who was on the phone, sir?"

"Quantico. They call me the moment anything comes in."

"Very smart, sir."

"What does it look like, Garcia?" Thomas and Garcia reached the bloody mess."

Four male bodies; all with shots to the head. One with multiple gunshot wounds. One bled out first before dying."

"Get to the fucking point, Garcia."

"It looks an awful lot like more of the Italian crime family drama The murder has to be from one of the rival families.

"My thoughts exactly, but something is off."

"What is it, sir?"

"The guards at the door and driver were finished off by one direct gunshot—clean kills. Our killer here is a marksman; he knew what he was doing. But this man, Andrea Saltinotti, died trying to get away. Have you read his record yet?"

"No sir, I didn't read get to that one."

"He's been the head of the Saltinottis for the past 8 years. Narcotics, human trafficking, booze, counterfeits—you name it: he runs it. Word on the street was he was planning to take over the imports from the harbor."

"The Giulianis."

"Yes, but look closely at Andrea. He has three bullet entries. Any one of these could've killed him if given time, but the killer decided to see him suffer. Look at the blood trail up to the doors."

Thomas nodded walking around the crime scene, making a mental map of the area and picturing the scene through the killer's eyes.

"The killer probably came behind those dumpsters." Agent Miller crouched over and patted Andrea's tuxedo, finding a folded piece of paper. He withdrew it from the dead man's front pocket and unfolded it, reading it a few times over.

"Garcia, take a look." he said, handing the bloodied paper to the other agent.

"Doesn't this look like a deal over the harbor?"

"Apparently, sir. It looks like the Lombardis had an agreement with the Saltinottis."

"It looks like more a sell-out by the Salinities to me."

"Why would the Lombardis want to sell their hold on the harbor to their rival?"

"It would be stupid to kill him after making a deal."

"My money's on the Giulianis."

"Maybe they're sending a message?"

"Just like they did with Terry."

"Let's wait for ballistics."

"Should I leave the bullets with forensics?"

"No, I'm having the evidence sent straight to Quantico. I don't want anyone except those with my explicit permission handling these crime scenes from now on."

Garcia crept over the body while Thomas shaded her, allowing her to pick up the bullet without being noticed. She then left the scene and waited in the car.

An officer approached Thomas Miller. "Sir, this young man here says he saw something." A child, around the age of ten, was dressed in his pajamas.

Thomas found it strange being that it was only 1 PM in the afternoon. Thomas crouched over looking at the boy. "Hello there, young man." The officer left, leaving them alone. "What's your name?" "I—Isaac," the boy said shyly. "I'm Thomas. Nice to meet you, Isaac." Thomas patted the boy softly on the head. "Did you see who did this?" The boy nodded; his eyes glued on the ground while he was hugging a small teddy bear. "Can you describe the bad man for me?" The boy nodded again. "H—he had on a white suit," the boy stuttered. "Where were you when the man did this?" The boy turned around, pointing to a window on the third floor of his home.

"What were you doing sitting there?"

The boy lifted his teddy bear.

"Were you sick today, playing with your teddy bear?"

The boy nodded.

"Can you describe this bad man in a white suit?" The

boy moved his head left and right, indicating he couldn't. "What did the man do after that?" "He ran away." the boy pointed in the direction. Thomas stood up patting the boy on the head. "Thank you for your service, young man." The officer returned to take the boy away.

Thomas walked to car and radioed Garcia. "Garcia, overnight send the bullet to Quantico. I have a lead to follow." "Ok, sir." Agent Garcia then pulled off.

Thomas later returned to his office at the 5th precinct, and spent the next hour or so searching the precinct's database for every property owned or controlled by the Giulianis near the crime scene. He found a few warehouses in the area and at least two apartment buildings nearby that were identified as Giuliani controlled properties. He thought they would probably be safehouses or storage for their illegal trades. There was also, Castello di Vino listed under Luca Giuliani's name. Without much time for getting warrants based on circumstantial evidence, Agent Miller decided to take his chances by visiting the pub.

18

A HUGE MESS

Giuliani Family and the FBI

Thomas drove an officer's car to Castello di Vino, parking across from the old castle-like pub. He got out and ran across the street, avoiding speeding cars beeping their horns. He entered the poorly lit Italian pub. The door slammed behind him, the bells overhead chiming frantically. Thomas immediately recognized a man dressed in white, with a glass of wine in his hand, sitting across from the bartender.

Thomas remained calm, cataloguing the exits. He didn't expect to find Francesco Giuliani so easily but if he had to kill the man, he was ready to do so. He just wanted to keep the casualties to a minimum: one. As if they could read his thoughts, the bartender and the man in the suit turned around.

"Ciao! May I help you signore?"

"Thomas Miller, FBI!" Thomas flashed his badge. Feigning ignorance, he said, "Are you Francesco Giuliani?"

"Si, that's me," Francesco said arrogantly.

"Mr. Federico," Thomas said, reading the barkeep's nametag, "please allow us to use this room privately. We have some business to discuss."

Francesco was finishing his third glass of wine when Thomas pulled up a stool beside him. Fredrico busied himself in the wine cellar.

"To what do I owe this pleasure, Agent Miller?"

"I know about your little rendezvous at the Saltinotti Mansion earlier." Francesco refilled his glass, emptying the bottle.

"Saltinotti Mansion ? Doesn't ring a bell." Francesco said, sipping his wine with abandon.

"Where were you this morning, Francesco? Let me guess, you've been here all day, drinking and the bartender is your alibi."

"You're excellent at your job, detective." he said in a condescending tone. "I was here, and Signore Federico will tell you the same."

"So, I guess you haven't heard that Andrea Saltinotti was murdered"

"Who's that guy you're referring to, again?" Now Francesco was messing with him.

Thomas sighed, but played along. "The head of the Saltinottis. He just finished a deal with the Lombardis to get your ports."

"This is the first time in my life I heard the names of those families, detective; I swear. You must have me mistaken."

"Funny you should say that. We have a witness." Francesco raised his eyebrows at his statement.

"Who might that be?"

"Should I tell you? They'll be dead along with your paid police staff, Terry and Jonathan."

"Who are these gentlemen you are mentioning?" Francesco continued to sip his wine. It was beyond him that Miller had found him here. He already knew too much, but he clearly didn't come to arrest him. He figured this meeting was coincidence and he'd see how long this would play out.

"Let's say we buried them not long ago. I was hoping you'd come to give your respects."

"I can't go to a stranger's funeral, Mr. Miller."

"That's a shame you think of them as strangers, because they wanted to confess about their ties with you." Thomas kept pushing but he had no solid proof. Francesco wasn't calling his bluff. "The witness we have placed you at the scene of the crime. And look at that, you're still wearing the white suit the witness described. You Giulianis sure are getting sloppy. The headline is already being printed, Francesco." Thomas said, waving his hand overhead as if he could see the headlines already. "And we have a match for the gun that killed Jonathan and Terry. It's the same weapon that was used to kill Davide Baldinotti." While Thomas kept talking,

Francesco's face turned pale. He almost matched his white suit. He screwed everything up by losing control of his quick temper.

"Am I under arrest, agent?" Francesco hands were sweaty and his guilt could be seen by his facial movements. "No, you're not at the moment but that can change. I don't want just you. I want all of you. You, gangsters, have caused me so much trouble for years, that when I get all of you, you'll be begging for your lives back." Thomas Miller hoped for a confession; scaring Francesco until admitting his role. For the first time, he was the underdog. "I don't know what you're talking about, Agent Miller, these families, you speak of."

"This is your only chance, Francesco. Cut the crap, give me what I want and you'll get immunity."

"I can't offer you something I don't have."

"Then, you're fucked. I know enough about you, Giulianis and thanks to Andrea's death, God rest his soul —if I can say that— he was a bad man— I have enough to take you all down; you and the Giulianis, the Lombardis, the Baldinottis, and the Saltinottis."

"What are you talking about, Agent?"

"You look tense, Francesco."

"I'm not."

"You're feeling the heat."

"I'm telling you, I'm not."

"The Lombardis sold their souls to the Saltinottis. Will you?" Francesco's hands began shaking underneath the table like a person with Parkinson's disease. He reached up for his glass of wine.

"Do you know what Saltinotti's death means for the deal between the Lombardis?"

"What does it mean, Agent?"

"They get nothing. Andrea's daughter in France will be in town to collect. Your businesses will close and New York will be in an all-out war."

Francesco remained silent as Agent Miller got up, placing his hat on his head. "I'll let you sleep on my offer, Francesco. Every hour that passes, I'll be closer to taking you down. Remember that. One fuck up will bring you all down. And don't even think about turning tail to Italy."

"If I'm the man you say I am, why should I not kill you right here and now?"

Thomas chuckled opening his shirt, revealing a wire. "Our little conversation. Of course, it might not be admissible in court, but if you kill me, everyone will know." Thomas buttoned up his shirt and walked off. Francesco knew the cable was nothing but a prop, helping Thomas bluff his way out just in case things went sour. But on the off chance the agent was telling the truth, he decided to play it safe.. Just when he thought he had recovered from the broken deal with Saltinottis, this bombshell hit him. Miller was right, he had gotten sloppy. The only thing Francesco that had gone right in the past few months was the Lombardi girl.

"There is still time. Consider my offer, Francesco.

Don't screw things up, again." The words of Agent Thomas Miller echoed around in his head, again and again.

Federico returned from the wine cellar and put his arm on Francesco's shoulder, squeezing it softly. He hadn't really been in the cellar all that time, and had instead been eavesdropping on Francesco's conversation with the agent.

"Scusa Francesco, this is a big mess."

"I know, Federico. I fucked up."

"I'm afraid you did."

"What should I do now?"

"Tell your father right away. Maybe he has already heard."

"He'll kill me and he will be right in doing so."

"It's a mess for sure but look at it as a learning curve. Everyone has hiccups."

"No, not like I do. I need to talk to Jessica." Francesco grabbed his coat and made his way to the exit.

"Grazie, Federico."

"Don't worry, my friend. We're still on top."

"That is my worry, Federico." Francesco left in anticipation of a dinner date with Jessica later that evening.

19

ANOTHER NIGHT AT THE HOTEL

Lombardi and Giuliani Family

Jessica was sitting alone in the living room, enjoying a burger with fries, watching one of her favorite TV shows. The TV was on, but her mind was roaming. A miracle that a man she felt closer was a man she'd never expect him to be. She picked up a fry, twisting it around, before eating it. She was more excited she'd meet Francesco than all the other times.

This time, they were going to stay at one of the top hotels in the city. The two had been going out for a few weeks, sometimes spending almost their entire nights out in hotel rooms, seeing the city, and enjoying each other's company. Before daybreak, they would sneak home. The two were forced to keep their relationship hidden and only Jessica's grandmother knew. Every time Francesco and Jessica met— it was more thrilling than the previous. With every new secret rendezvous, they realized they'd completed each other.

No one was at home at the Lombardi Mansion beside the groundskeepers. Giovanni woke Jessica up early before leaving. A few weeks ago, she would have lashed out at him for ruining her precious sleep. Lately, she's been able to sleep well. At the beginning of each day, she started off jogging, and then after breakfast, she'd look over her cases. She often daydreamed about Francesco while working but around by midday, she was interrupted by the phone ringing. Skipping from joy to it, she answered.

"Hello?"

"Jessica, it's me."

"Francesco!" she said almost a little too enthusiastically. She tried again, "Hi. How are you?"

"I need to see you. "he said.

"Are you alright?"

"Yes! I miss you so much."

"You couldn't wait until evening, huh?"

He could hear her smirk through the phone. "No, I can't. I need you to come meet me right away. Are you busy?"

"No, I'm not. I'll get ready to meet you. You sure you're alright?"

"Yes, sweetheart. I am. I'll be waiting."

Jessica hung up excited, but she felt a slight pain in her calf; a cramp which clawed its way from the calf to her thigh that made her groan. She moved her leg around, before limping her way to her room.

* * *

After feeling better and getting dressed, Jessica called for a taxi to take her to the Plaza Hotel, their usual meeting spot for lunch. She waited in the lobby, donning her sunglasses and fixing herself in the mirror before proceeding to reception. A young woman, with black hair, greeted Jessica.

"Hello Miss, how may I help you?"

"I'm expecting someone for a meeting."

"Can I have a name please?"

"Of course, it's Timothy Barn."

"Room 503."

"Thank you."

"You're welcome. Enjoy your stay."

Jessica went to the elevators and pressed the up arrow. It was a shame they had to use an alias to see one another but Jessica knew if her father found out, the city was a graveyard.

Jessica tapped on the door and Francesco opened it, only wearing a pair of boxers. His abs turned Jessica on. She jumped into his arms, embracing and kissing him.

"I missed you, honey," Jessica said before kissing Francesco again.

"I missed you, too" He held her tightly, but it seemed insincere.

Jessica walked inside, heading for the minibar, pouring herself a gin. She sat on a leather couch across the king-size bed.

"Is everything alright?"

Francesco was pondering what to say. She never saw him look so worried but waited for him to answer.

"Yeah, everything's fine."

Jessica set her glass down with a light clink on the bar top. Francesco had taken a seat at the foot of the bed and she climbed on, beside him. She weaved her hand into his and squeezed it, softly. slowly removing her clothes. She wanted Francesco to take her again like he had done every time they met.

"I think there's something you're not, Francesco. Should I be worried?" She waited a few beats for his answer and wrapped her arms around him, kissing him softly on the neck.

"No, everything's fine, really." It wasn't the answer she'd wanted. She cupped his face between her palms and made him face her.

"You know you can trust me."

"I know." He said, looking down and fidgeting with the silken drawstring of his boxers.

"Then what's wrong?"

"Business bullshit."

"Business bullshit that has you agitated."

"I fucked up."

"What happened now, baby?"

"I—"

"There's nothing you can say that will change how I feel."

"How do you feel?"

"I love you, Francesco if you wanted to know."

That was the first time Jessica said those words. Francesco hadn't expected her to confess her love then and there, but he couldn't deny he'd felt the same, ever since they'd first met, he'd been drawn to her. It didn't make things any easier, though. The murder he'd committed today, the detective's brazen warning, and now Jessica's love had him confused. Francesco smiled for the first time all day.

"I love you too, Jess."

"Then what is it, sweetheart?"

"I killed somebody today."

She wasn't surprised that this was his news. She didn't like it, but it was part of their lives whether they liked it or not, and the least she could do was be there for him.

"It's not the first time."

"No, but today it was wrong."

"Was he innocent?"

"No, not at all."

"Then why are you upset?"

"I ruined our families by doing so." Francesco scrubbed his hand through his unruly, dark hair, making it stick up in places. Jessica could tell he was exhausted.

Jessica stepped back and sat over on the dark leather couch.

"Come here, Francesco, tell me what happened." Francesco came over, passing his hand through her hair.

"I killed Andrea Saltinotti."

"My brother was there to meet him this morning."

"I saw Giovanni as he was leaving."

"Then?"

"It was just Andrea and a few men."

"What's the problem, then?"

"There was a witness."

"What?"

"An FBI agent came to Castello earlier and told me."

"And?"

"They have nothing substantial, Jess but they know everything."

"If he has nothing, then there's nothing to worry about."

"They'll figure it out eventually."

"We can worry about that later."

Jessica climbed onto Francesco's lap and faced him. She leaned in and planted warm kisses on his lips, her soft hands moving up and down his bare chest. They kept kissing, occasionally breaking for air and conversation.

"Have you ever thought of leaving this all behind?" Jessica said.

"All the time." he groaned in reply.

"Why don't we just go then?" Jessica said making a trail of kisses from his ear down to his neck.

"I can't. Not yet" Francesco moaned softly, pulling Jessica closer. Their bodies were so sinfully close.

"When this is all over?" she kept kissing down his chest.

"When the job is done, yes."

Francesco lifted her and carried her to the bed.

They spent the rest of the afternoon making out and enjoying one another's company. Nothing else was on their minds. time seemed to stop only for them.

Later, they spent the evening in bed, with Jessica sleeping on Francesco's chest while he watched TV. The news coverage of the Saltinotti murder was brief and he was glad.

Francesco turned off the TV set and within minutes, their snores echoed the silence of the large hotel room.

* * *

The next morning, Francesco woke up first and headed for the shower, trying not to wake Jessica. He called for room service and ordered breakfast. Jessica woke up from the sound of the door opening.

"Yes, thank you very much. Here's something for you." Francesco closed it, bringing inside a tray.

Jessica sat up half-naked and went to Francesco smiling.

"Good morning." She kissed him before heading to the bathroom.

"Good morning," he said putting the tray down. After Jessica showered, they had breakfast together.

Jessica took a sip of coffee, resting her legs on Francesco's lap.

"What will we do today?"

"It's been a while since we went to Castello."

"Indeed! I'd love to have an afternoon gin."

"You are an alcoholic, you know that?"

"Says that guy who drinks nonstop at 11 AM!"

"That was a long time ago."

"It wasn't that long ago."

"Whatever."

"And I'm sure you'd go drinking right now if you weren't with me."

"What can I say? I love my wine."

"And I love gin," Jessica said smirking as she gazed into Francesco's eyes. She couldn't take them off him. She moved her legs, pushing Francesco's legs playfully, but then felt another cramp, making her grunt.

"What's wrong?"

"I got a cramp," she said moving her legs about, trying to find a position that wouldn't hurt.

"Where does it hurt, baby?" Francesco moved his hands from Jessica's calf to her thighs. "Right there." Jessica pointed and Francesco started massaging that area. Jessica put her cup of coffee on the table and laid back as Francesco turned her pain to pleasure.

Francesco kept stroking while leaning in for a kiss every few seconds.

"I guess we have a little bit of time left before we leave."

"I think so." Jessica moaned with pleasure as his hands went further up.

They spent two more hours making out then hastily got dressed and left; leaving their breakfast on the table untouched. Francesco and Jessica made their way through the hotel lobby as the bellhop brought their scant luggage down.

"So, 6 PM at the Castello?"

"Sounds good." Francesco grabbed Jessica and kissed her goodbye as her taxi arrived.

20

THE HAPPY NEWS

Lombardi Family

Jessica returned home to find no one was in the front area. Everyone was still out. Jessica for the last few weeks told them she was studying at the downtown library for her bar exam. Her mother and father sensed something else was going on but didn't want to intrude. Her mother always told her to find someone whom she'd love as well as her parents. Little did they know that it was the son of their most hated enemy. In the meantime, her grandmother kept her promise and Jessica was grateful.

When Jessica entered the kitchen, she heard the TV on in the guest room. She crept softly down the hallway, seeing her grandmother alone on the couch, watching Happy Days.

"Grandma!" Jessica called as she went to hug her.

"Nipotina! What time is it?"

"I was out a little later than usual."

"With Francesco again?"

"Shhh!"

"Everyone's out. Don't worry."

"Yes, with him again and it was amazing."

"I can see it on your face."

As Jessica sat, she had another cramp, near her stomach, making her lie back.

"Stai bene?"

"Yes, it's just a spasm."

"How long has this been happening?"

"How long, what?"

"You are having spasms."

"About a week or so."

Her grandmother paused, thinking.

"I want to ask you something, but do not panic."

"What?" Jessica coaxed already anxious.

"Have you had your period yet?" Jessica gasped putting her hand on her mouth.

"Umm, I'm two days late."

"Maybe you should take the pregnancy test."

Jessica giggled but she was unsure.

"I am not pregnant, Grandma."

"You might be, Nipotina."

"How?"

"If you have sex, you can carry a child."

"No, I mean, how do you figure I might be?"

"I had those spasms when that nasty father of yours was inside me."

Jessica was astonished by what her grandmother just told her.

"Go lie down. I'll make sure nobody knows of this. You need to rest right now." Her grandmother stood up, heading for the door.

"Grandma, I'm not pregnant," Jessica whispered.

"You lie down and we'll find out soon." Her grandmother grabbed her purse and left after one of the guards came.

* * *

An hour later, her grandmother returned, seeing Jessica still sitting in the same spot. "Jessica?" The old woman called with compassion. Jessica turned around slowly. Her eyes were swollen and red and her makeup had been smeared by her tears.

"Yes?"

"Siete pronti?" Her grandmother took a seat next to her.

"Si, I am ready. I guess." Jessica shrugged.

"Here is the test, Nipotina. I'll be here."

Jessica smiled but she really didn't want to. She headed to the bathroom. "I'll be back, nonna. Thank you."

She stood up over the toilet after pulling down her dress. Then, she opened the device. "This is the moment of truth," she sighed to herself, afraid of the outcome. If it was positive, she didn't know what she'd do. She could only hide it for so long, and if her parents ever found out that Francesco was the father, they'd likely hate the baby as much as they hate the Giuliani's already. placed it inside.

* * *

Minutes later, she ran to her grandmother and hugged her.

"It says positive," Jessica collapsed in her grandmother's arms, her body wracked with sobs. Her grandmother held her tightly.

"Finalmente!" Jessica gave her grandmother a puzzled look.

"W—why are you so happy? This is a curse!"

"Sta'zitto Nipotina! This is a great blessing!"

"But—"

"No buts, Jessica. What greater joy than a little bambino running around here?"

"My father will kill us."

"If he lays a finger on my Jessica, or my great grandbaby, I will cut his braccio! You hear me?"

"Everyone will be angry. They will call me a traitor."

"Oh, your grandmother always wanted a pronipote! What a blessing!"

Jessica couldn't believe her grandmother. The old woman was so happy, yet Jessica was scared for her life. Slowly, as she watched her grandmother ramble about this and that, her worries turned to snippets of comfort.

"I'll be a mother!"

"A madre!"

"I'll be a mother! I can't believe this," Jessica laughed wiping her tears which kept running down her face. Her grandmother palmed Jessica's face and wiped her tears off with her thumbs.

"Now, this is the face of a mother."

"Thank you."

"Thank your partner," her grandmother chuckled, making Jessica laugh awkwardly.

The couple went to the living room, laughing, both with tears.

"Go tell your future husband!"

"I'll tell him tonight when we meet again."

"You'll need a home and we must find a good church."

"Slow down, grandma. One thing at a time."

"If it's a girl, I hope you give it my name."

"Serena Lombardi?"

"Oh, that sounds wonderful."

"It does, doesn't it?" Jessica smiled and hugged her grandmother again. "I have to get ready. Thank you, grandma." Jessica laughed again.

"Stop thanking me," joked her grandmother, patting Jessica on the head.

"Please, don't say anything to anyone."

"Nipotina, get out of here. Your nonna isn't stupid. Go and get ready." Serena guided Jessica playfully out of the room.

21

THE PRODIGAL SON

The Giuliani Family

Francesco was heading back to the Giuliani Mansion . He wanted to first go by Castello's, but he knew he had to face his father, Luca. The consequences of his actions weighed down heavily on him as he drove through the streets of New York.

Once he arrived, he pushed open the iron gates, ignoring the guards who greeted him. He made his way to the front entrance; through the yard. Each step weighed heavier and heavier on Francesco. He wanted to get this over with, so he could go on and meet Jessica.

Francesco opened the front door, finding his brother coming downstairs.

"Good evening, Manuel!" Francesco said only receiving a stone-cold look from his brother as he came over.

"Dad knows what you did. You fucked up," he whispered.

"What are you talking about?"

"I heard about everything yesterday. You killed all these people."

"Dad said that?"

"Come on, bro. Everybody in town knows."

"That's not true."

"You're a fucking liar. I'm glad I don't look up to you anymore."

"What, you little fuck—?"

"You heard me."

"That's not the way you talk to your older brother, Manuel!"

"That's how I talk to a murderer!"

Francesco snapped grabbing Manuel by the shirt and twisted his arm.

"Say it again and I'll break this little arm of yours, smart ass."

"You heard me. I said you're a murderer!" Manuel said in pain, but brazen.

"You will show me some respect!" Francesco shouted as his brother's cries from the pain echoed the halls of the mansion .

From the top of the stairs, the boys heard their father clearing his throat.

"Let him go, Francesco." Francesco saw his father, towering an entire story over them. He released Manuel with a shove, who stomped out of the room, coddling his arm.

"My office, now." his father bellowed as he stormed down the stairs. Francesco knew he was in more trouble than ever.

Luca sat behind his desk and made a gesture, telling Francesco to sit across from him. There was a rage in Luca's eyes; Francesco knew at any moment, he'd lash out and start shouting. Francesco crossed his legs and returned the Don's low stare.

"What the hell were you thinking, Francesco?" he finally said.

"About what?"

"Hurting your brother?"

"He called me a murderer!"

"So? You're not?"

"Everyone in this family is."

"What's wrong with you?"

"What, father?"

"You just tried to hurt your only brother?"

"No, I just—"

"Is this the way I raised you?"

"No, father."

"When you started in my business, what did I first tell you?"

"The streets are the streets."

"You don't bring the streets inside this home!"

"I just—"

"Shut up. I'm talking now. You've been reckless with Davide, then you kill two of *our* policemen. I gave you one simple order, Francesco, no more killings, especially not made men. And what do you do? Exactly what I told you not to—you go and kill Andrea Saltinotti and his driver!"

"He was talking bad about the family, father!"

"So, what? Do we kill a made man because of his mouth? Is that the way we built our business? Is this the Italian way?"

"We must clean house, father."

"Clean house? Not by killing the made men in the city, Francesco. Where's the honor in that? You may have killed us. Our colleagues in Italy are going to lose business and that means one thing."

"Where are these families in honoring us, Giulianis?"

"Andrea was a stand-up guy and a friend!"

"Was he, father?"

"Si, Francesco. I agree, Davide deceived us, and Andrea just needed a little convincing."

"So, was that *honor*, father?"

"It is more honorable than what you have done, my son!"

"I—"

"Don't say anything else?"

Luca took a deep breath to calm himself down.

"I think you need a break from the business, son."

"What, father? No, not now."

"Don't argue with me, Francesco. This stuff is destroying you."

"I have things under control. No one will fuck us over."

"No, you don't. Look at what you have become—a hitman? My son is not a goddamn hitman."

"I'm not, father!"

Francesco stood up and kissed his father's hand before heading for the door.

"When was the last time you went to church, Francesco? Have you confessed your sins?" Luca yelled after him. Francesco paused, reflecting on the last few weeks in the business. His father taught him to pray and ask for forgiveness for each sin when he was younger and while they weren't devout Catholics, they were religious. Yet another aspect of his life he'd disappoint his father with. Francesco remembered praying at Davide's execution but he hadn't prayed for Andrea. Now, it's come back to haunt him. Francesco turned around and looked at his father, feeling guilty.

"Father, you're right." Francesco came back and sat down beside his father. "I'm sorry."

"Francesco, I worry about you."

"I know you do, father. It's just—"

"Please, no more excuses. You screwed up and it will take some fixing, but things will be okay."

"I fucked up."

"Yet, I'm more concerned about this family, inside my home."

"I know, father."

"Son, honestly, I'm losing my love for running the

business. We have enough legal businesses to call it quits. If it's over for me, it'll probably for the Giulianis."

"I can't accept that, father."

"This is my fault. You don't have the makeup of the men of old back home. You were raised in America. Us, old-timers always did business discreetly."

Francesco stayed silent. Everything around him was collapsing. His desire to uphold his family's honor was slowly chipping away like paint on an old car.

"I… have to go, father." Francesco opened the door and left to meet up with the one good thing that he still had—Jessica Lombardi.

22

THE HIT

The Lombardi and Giuliani Family

Francesco had spent an hour at Castello di Vino, talking with his dear friend, Federico. He had already finished a bottle and was on his second.

"Slow down my friend," Federico said smiling.

"It's ok. I need to take some things off my mind."

"Did your father rip you?"

"Worse."

"Worse?"

"He was right about everything."

"Like what?"

"This business. It has changed me."

"I can't argue with that."

"You see it, too?"

"For a long time."

"Why didn't you say anything?"

"You'll die in the business with honor which would be the only way I've known you."

"Oh, fuck you, Federico."

"Now, you have come to your senses—"

"That, indeed, has happened."

"You're stubborn to stay stuck in the old ways?"

"I was."

Federico opened another bottle and filled two glasses.

"That one is on the house."

"Isn't everything in the house for me?"

"I have a tab on you. You owe me molti soldi. This is Luca's money."

Francesco laughed raising his glass. "To a new man. To my old friend," Federico raised his an took a sip.

* * *

Jessica was almost ready to go to Castello di Vino. She was nervous about telling him about her pregnancy but being there with Federico would make things less tense. She put on her light blue summer dress and rushed downstairs. Taking a final look in the mirror, she heard her brother Giovanni shouting from Michael's office.

"I want that fucker dead!" His rant was far enough for her to not hear exactly what was going on. Jessica didn't want to get involved and opened the front door. Her cab was waiting outside, and the bodyguards opened the door for her to get in.

The cab driver was professional; he didn't try making

small talk. Jessica stared out the window, watching the busy New York nightlife blur by as the drive sped her to her destination. The weather forecast predicted heavy rains. For Jessica, she didn't care about the weather. She paid more attention to the people having dinner, rushing back home from work. The Chinese were out in front arranging the merchandise of their shops. Jessica lowered the cab's window and the sweet smell of rain filled her nostrils.

The rain got heavier by the time Jessica arrived at Castello's. She took a deep breath and tried hiding her smile but she was undoubtably nervous. She entered, seeing Francesco and Federico talking and laughing. It was a scene that warmed her heart, starring the man she was in love with.

She ran behind Francesco, wrapping her arms around his neck and kissing him on the cheek like a little girl.

"Hey, you!"

"Hi, Federico!"

"Signorina! Welcome back!" Federico said excitedly to see her. Francesco turned, grabbing Jessica, giving her a deep kiss. Federico's eyebrows raised.

"I see you're already drinking without me."

"We had had a few glasses together."

"A few bottles he means."

"And weren't you the one nagging me about gin?"

"I didn't say I wouldn't drink it."

"Ok."

"You seem very… excited."

"I missed you!"

"I did, too." Francesco kissed her again. Jessica then took a seat next to Francesco. She sat as close as possible, practically lying on his shoulder. Her body faced completely toward him, almost disregarding Federico. Francesco held her hands in his and stared into her eyes. Federico served Jessica a glass of gin and stood there, awkwardly admiring the scene of his two friends in love. Jessica took a sip but spat it back into the glass.

"Francesco—," she began, scrambling for the right words.

"Jessica?"

"I have something to tell you."

"Is it good or bad?"

"Very good."

"Good. I could use some good news."

"I mean excellent news, actually."

"I knew there was something behind that smile."

"There is."

"What is it, my love?"

"Promise me you won't get mad or leave me."

"Why would I leave you?"

"Together we are?"

"Together, we are."

"Okay," Jessica breathed a sigh, steeling herself. "Remember the spasms I had yesterday?"

"Yes, I was the one massaging them."

"They weren't just spasms."

"Oh, well, is everything ok?"

"Yes, my love."

"Well, what is Jessica tell me."

"I'm pregnant."

Francesco swallowed hard. He didn't know what to think of what Jessica had just told him. His stomach churned and he felt sweat prickle on his skin. A feeling of nervousness crept into his mind until finally giving its place to unexplainable joy. He was going to be a father. What were the Lombardis and Giulianis going to do? Francesco's jaw dropped and his body went rigid at the thought. He tried speaking but words wouldn't come out. There was an awkward silence until Federico whooped and hollered out of joy and excitement.

"I'm going to be a zio!" He cheered, scrambling up his creaky, wooden step-stool and reaching for a bottle of fine whiskey from the top shelf.

Francesco hugged Jessica tightly and tears streamed down their faces in rivulets. He couldn't believe it.

"I—I don't know what to say," he said wiping his face.

"Say, you love me. That's enough."

"I love you. I love you!" he shouted, massaging her belly. The few customers in the pub congratulated them by raising their glasses.

"Together," Jessica said with tears.

"Together." Francesco hugged her again.

Federico poured three shots and pushed two of them towards Jessica and Francesco.

"Drink now, because in a few months you will not be able to."

"You're amazing, Federico." Jessica raised her glass, unsure. "Are you sure about me drinking?"

"It's the tradition. Look at the men around."

"Then, to family!" Jessica raised her glass.

"To family!" Federico and Francesco cheered, tossing back their shots. Federico filled their glasses once more.

"These are on the house as well, Francesco." Federico chuckled.

"I thought everything was on the house." Jessica giggled.

"Oh no, I'm keeping a tab on you as well, Signorina. I might even open a tab for the little one." Federico said, gesturing at Jessica's belly as he kept pouring.

* * *

The three were drinking and laughing throughout the evening. Francesco often found himself staring into Jessica's eyes. The thought of family, living together, raising their child away from New York and the business was a sign from God. It was the sign Francesco needed to leave everything behind and repent for his sins.

"You make me so happy."

"I was afraid at first."

"Why?"

"You might be against having a child."

"Oh, I would have killed Francesco myself, if he

refused, Jessica." Federico interrupted. Francesco laughed, rubbing his head.

"I would never be against anything to do with you. You know that."

"It's just—our families."

"Screw them."

"We are still at war."

"They'll have to accept it."

Jessica paused swirling her whiskey around in the tiny shot glass. The amber liquid reflected the pub's soft lighting and she felt warm inside for more than one reason. She was silent a moment and finally said, "Thank you."

"For what?"

"For making me a mother."

"You made me the happiest father alive."

"I love you."

"I love you, too." Francesco kissed Jessica and she snuggled up next to him. She felt safe and all of her insecurities fell softly and soundly to sleep in his arms.

* * *

Thunder boomed outside of the pub while the inside became increasingly quieter as the customers began to leave. Raindrops slicked down the windows like tears of joy. The streets were nearly empty with everyone rushing homeward from the heavy rain. But there was a black Chevrolet Tahoe with tinted black windows driving down the same street of Castello di Vino. The speeding vehicle resembled a wild animal, recklessly stalking its prey. When It stopped outside the pub, the driver lowered the windows. Castello's windows were shattered by bullets flying.

"Giu!" Federico yelled, ducking behind the counter. The bullets hit everything; shredding medieval decorations and shattering the wine bottles on the shelves. Francesco jumped up, tackling Jessica to the ground. The rapid gunfire and the ricochet of bullets and shrapnel made the once-peaceful pub look like a war zone.

The place looked like hell, with bullet holes dotting every square foot of the building's interior and rivers of booze and wine pooling on the floor. Finally, the gunfire came to a halt, the deafening silence giving way to the sound of a car screeching away on the wet pavement.

"Are you okay?" Francesco said to Jessica, still on top of her.

"We have to go, tonight," Jessica said shivering.

"Tonight," she said again, when Francesco didn't answer her. Tears slithered their way down her cheeks and she was shaking with adrenaline.

"Okay." Francesco stood up and went to look out the window, pulling out his gun.

"Federico, are you okay?" Francesco's ears were still ringing.

"I'm fine."

"Who were those guys?"

"I didn't see the car!"

"Fuck!"

"Who were they after?"

"Me, probably." Francesco went back to pull Jessica to her feet, patting the dust off from her dress.

"Francesco, I can't do this anymore.

"I know, my love."

"We have to leave now. Do you fucking hear me?"

"Yes."

"Non restero qui, con il padre del mio figlio essere cacciato come un animale selvaggio. Non retero qui avendo quelle famiglie del cazzo rovinare la mia vita e tutto cio che amo. Non tollerero rischiare mio bambino o mia felicita per una guerra familiare. Non Io faro…"

Francesco held Jessica in his arms. She was in a state of shock. For a moment, Francesco questioned his sanity and wanted swift retaliation but came back to his senses at the sight of a panicked Jessica.

"We're leaving. Relax, my love." Jessica couldn't bear another minute being at the pub. She pounded against Francesco's chest again and again.

"I want to go.." she said over and over.

Federico looked at Francesco. He was more concerned about Jessica than his friend.

"I have a plan, Francesco."

"No."

"Why not?"

"I don't want this news to reach home."

"It's over?"

"It's over."

"Are you sure, my friend?"

"This was more than enough of a wake-up call."

"Where are you going?"

"I don't know. I guess our first stop is the Greyhound."

"The bus? Why not Aeroporto?"

"With the FBI on us and now with whoever tried to kill us, it will be hard to leave undetected."

"I agree."

"I'll stop by one of our safehouses near the port."

"Is it stocked?"

"Yes, we have some cash, passports, and guns stashed there."

"Francesco, I'm sorry."

"For what?"

"I didn't shoot back."

"Federico, get it together."

"You could have been killed."

"So, could all of us. It's okay. Besides, you wouldn't have had a clear shot anyway. "

"I'm sorry, my friend. You are our Don's son. I've failed you," Federico kept grumbling, leaning against the counter.

* * *

Francesco, Federico, and Jessica were as devastated as the pub around them. The Lombardi girl, who left a life in Italy not long ago, to join her father's business was still shaking. When everything was falling in place so perfectly, this hit came and had hit her the hardest. It was harder than she expected.

Francesco grabbed her chin and forced her to look at him. Her eyes were red and her makeup was ruined.

"We're leaving now!"

"Hurry, please."

"We'll take the first bus."

"Where?

"Anywhere away from here."

"Together."

"Together."

"Give me a moment, sweetie. Go use the restroom and get freshened up. I need to talk to Federico." Francesco turned to Federico as Jessica left.

"Addio, amico mio." Francesco extended his arm towards Federico and they shook hands after embracing.

"Addio Francesco. Seguine il tuo cuore. May God keep you safe. I will tell Luca. You just go!"

In their escape, Jessica and Francesco sped past a black Chevrolet Tahoe parked just over a hundred meters from the pub but didn't know the men inside were responsible for the hit job. The driver hesitated to fire another shot when he realized Francesco wasn't alone. The couple continued running for close to fifteen minutes, without stopping to catch their breaths. The heavy rain whipped their faces, making it hard for them to see. When they reached a warehouse at the docks, Francesco pulled out a large set of keys and opened the lock. The rain pounded against the metal roof overhead, like drums of war as Francesco and Jessica stepped inside.

"We'll take a few things and be on our way." Francesco's voice echoed the empty warehouse as he read the tags on a few boxes. Jessica was still shivering but was feeling a bit better. "Here we are." Francesco opened a box, unveiling a packet of bills next to a black Adidas sweatshirt. He took off his white suit and got changed.

Jessica laughed but it was nice to see Francesco dressed in something more casual. He grabbed another box and dropped it on the ground. "I think we have something for you." The box read *Sofia Giuliani.* "Open it, sweetheart."

"Please, don't make me dress in an old woman's clothes."

"Don't worry. My mother has taste," chuckled Francesco.

Jessica opened the bag, finding various luxury makeup and cosmetics. She kept digging until she found a pair of black leggings and a white Fila sweatshirt. When she got changed, she almost matched Francesco.

"Hey, babe! This actually fits me."

"I see," Francesco mind drifted elsewhere as he looked her up and down. However, he remained focused, pulling out a few more things. Jessica looked through the makeup bag and began feeling better.

"I should change my look," said Jessica staring at Francesco.

"We don't have time, sweetheart."

Deciding, Jessica pulled out a pair of scissors and within minutes, cut her long hair to shoulder-length. Francesco watched her as she cut her hair and was impressed by how good her new hairstyle looked, all things considered.

"It brings your face out," he snickered, searching for something to hide his own hair.

"You think?" She grabbed a mirror from her handbag. "God, I'm hot."

Even with their lives in danger, Francesco and Jessica were cherishing their time together.

"Yes, you are, my Donna." Francesco planted a short kiss on Jessica's lips.

"Check out this Cincinnati Reds Hat." Francesco pulled it out of a box and put it on. The young Giuliani looked like an middle-school baseball coach.

"You love hats, don't you?"

"I always have since I was a little boy. But we need one last thing before we go." Francesco reached for a box that had 'I.D.' written on it and pulled out one from a stack. "My name now is John Papadakis."

"Oh, Mister Papadakis. Let me guess, I'm the newly-wed, Christina Papadakis?" Jessica wrapped her arms around Francesco and kissed him.

"That sounds nice. Mrs. Papadakis."

"I could get used to this name, Mr. Papadakis."

"Really?"

"I think so but only if you grew a mustache."

"Wow! Not a bad idea."

"Honey, please don't." She'd regretted the suggestion as soon as it escaped her lips.

"Honestly, I always wanted one."

"Let's just go."

"Ok."

* * *

Francesco gave Jessica a duffle bag with clothes while he grabbed another with cash.

They walked to the nearest bus station not far from the port and got tickets heading to Rockport, Maine. The bus was nearly empty and as soon as they took their seats, Jessica rested on Francesco's chest.

"We're are really leaving."

"Thank God!"

"It was a mistake getting involved my family's business."

"Well, we're both out of it."

"Honey, do you think we can buy a house by the beach?"

"With all the money we have, we can buy a mansion ."

"No more mansion s please, sweetheart."

"Then, a small home for us and the child."

"That sounds better."

"It does?"

"I should call my grandmother. She's going to be worried."

"It's a little early. Wait until we are at least out of New York."

"Ok, baby."

"Don't worry. You can call her from one of the rest-stops on the way."

"By the way, she wants us to name the child, Serena if it's a girl."

"What a beautiful name! Serena Papadakis."

"And if it's a boy?"

"Federico."

"Hmm! Federico Papadakis. That sounds funny."

Minutes later, Jessica fell asleep on Francesco's chest. She slept like a baby who was safe and sound. Francesco watched her until he also fell asleep.

23

BLOODSHED OVER NEW YORK

The Lombardi and Giuliani Family

The driver of the black Chevrolet saw Francesco and Jessica exiting the pub. He praised God he didn't kill the girl. Once he got back to the Lombardi Mansion , he was dripping wet from the rain, his rumpled hat in hand. His wet bald head and big red nose glistened in the dim light in Michael Lombardi's office. He stood opposite the Don, with his eyes glued to the floor out of respect and guilt. Sitting on a leather couch in the dark near the door, was Michael's son, Giovanni, polishing his Smith and Wesson Model 21.

The driver remained silent, waiting for Don Michael to speak. as the only sound to be heard in the grand room was the various clicking from Giovanni's gun-polishing and the driver's belabored breathing. Michael was reading a copy of the deal with Andrea Saltinotti, ignoring the driver who was waiting patiently until he was finished. Michael raised his head, finally acknowledging him as he took off his small reading glasses.

"So, is it done?"

"Boss, I have bad news—"

"Go on."

"Francesco's still alive."

"That's not what I ordered? Is it?"

"No, Don but there's something far worse."

"Does he know it was us?"

"I don't know but there is something you should know."

"Then speak!"

"He escaped Castello di Vino with your daughter."

"With my daughter? What was she doing in that shithole?"

"I waited outside and saw them leaving, Don."

"My daughter? Are you sure ? Are you fucking drunk?"

"No, Don. I haven't taken a drink today. I saw the Giuliani boy with your daughter." the driver repeated.

"So, my daughter, Jessica was inside the Giuliani pub?"

"Yes, sir."

"And you shot the place up?"

"Sir, I didn't—"

"You shot up the place with my fucking daughter inside?"

"Don, I was just—"

"What the hell was Jessica doing there in the first place?"

"I don't know, Don."

"You mean, you didn't follow them before you shot up the damn place, you fucking idiot?"

"I—I didn't know, Don."

"Out, Now!" Michael slammed his fists on his desk. The driver rushed out, leaving the door open. Michael turned to Giovanni.

"Set up a meeting with Luca!" said the Don holding his forehead in despair.

"When, father?"

"Yesterday, goddamit! When? Right now! Your sister could be kidnapped by those savages!" Michael's voice echoed down the hall even as Giovanni descended the stairs.

* * *

Michael spent time alone in his office, pacing and waiting for Luca to respond to his invitation. His wife tried to comfort him but he sent her off. A part of the old Don felt sorry for the way he treated Jessica, but his feelings of remorse never conquered his rage for the Giulianis. Wrecking his deal with Andrea was dishonorable, but this was more pressing. It required immediate action before the city would fall into an all-out war.

Two hours later, Don Luca Giuliani entered Michael's office, soaked from the rain. The low lighting and his slim figure made him look tired. His men were waiting out front and the Don honestly didn't know what the meeting was called for. Michael sat behind his desk with a look of authority. With a simple hand gesture, he had pointed to one of the chairs and Luca took a seat.

"Ciao, Michael," Luca said before sitting.

"Ciao, Luca."

"You wanted to meet."

"Yes, we must talk. This is urgent."

"If this is about Andrea, I'm afraid I have nothing to say."

"No, this isn't about Andrea."

"Then what?"

"Luca, I respect you, you know. You, Giulianis, were in charge of this city for many years but—"

"Thank you, Michael, but cut the bullshit. What do you want?"

"Please allow me to speak, Luca. I respect you as my big brother with honor. You were in charge like a king. What happened?"

"I'm retiring soon, Michael. Others can take over."

"So, that means you can do as like? What's happened to your honor among our families, Luca?"

"What are you saying, Michael?"

"First with Davide."

"He betrayed the Omerta."

"Bene. Then, Andrea."

"I told you, I don't have anything to say about that."

"Yet, there was no honor in how made men get killed without consulting back home."

"I agree with you, Michael. My son has been reckless. He's still learning the ropes."

"And now my daughter?"

"What are you saying?"

"You heard me, Luca. Your son's meddling in my territory!"

"What are you talking about?"

"I'll ask once, Luca, out of respect. Where's my daughter?"

"I don't know what you're implying. Is she missing?"

"That idiot son of yours kidnapped her!"

"That's ridiculous."

"My men have seen them running off like two bandits that robbed a bank! Where's my daughter, Michael?"

"I haven't seen my son since this morning."

"Luca, I respect you but this has gone far enough."

"What do you want from me? I don't have your daughter, Michael. Why would you insinuate such a thing? Our families' blood is sacred."

"Don't come in my office lying to my face,"

"Yes, we have our differences, but I wouldn't hurt your family."

"You're out of line, Luca; you and that figlio del cazzo of yours. I could have had him killed."

"Michael, you are not thinking straight, and you don't want to go there.

"This is an act of war, Luca. Remember my words. When this is over, there would be only one family in New York."

"Michael, I urge you not to do something you'll regret."

"Get out of my office, Luca. Now! Out!"

Luca took a deep breath and walked with his men to where his driver was waiting with the engine still on. Before Luca climbed into the backseat, he told his men to find Francesco immediately.

* * *

For weeks, New York turned into a war zone as the Lombardi families and their allies unleashed their rage against the Giulianis. Francesco and Jessica were long gone and the Lombardis swore to tear the city apart, until Jessica was found, or the Giulianis were completely wiped out.

At first, the war was one-sided since Luca refused to go to war. The Lombardis sided with the remaining fractions of the Saltinottis and the Baldinottis whom all aligned in hate against the Giulianis. They raided their businesses one by one, hindering gun and liquor sales. The harbors were taken by force; pier by pier causing the revenue for the Giulianis to drop. As a result, the Giulianis stopped offering protection to the Chinese shops which were a large part of their profits. The shop owners were now forced to pay taxes and pay for protection to the Lombardis.

The town of New York devolved into an Italian ghetto, which its citizens avoided at night. Every mom-and-pop shop that once belonged to the Giulianis was ransacked. The small pubs were set on fire, oftentimes resulting in senseless fatalities. New York's police precincts were given overtime to combat the violence but many on the force were getting paid by the Lombardis and their allies. They made arrests on anyone connected to the Giulianis. The detectives searched home by home, in search of Jessica Lombardi and still no luck. Michael spent days inside his office having back-to-back meetings with police captains and loyal family members and allies, discussing their next move. His son, Giovanni was out in the streets, leading small units for raids and executions.

New York was bathed in blood. The constant smell of fire and gun smoke on every corner was on display on TV News channels across the country. *"The Bloodshed over New York"*, became the national headline. The Mayor and City Council never expected in New York's history something of this magnitude happening.

They urged New York's citizens to stay inside and to go out only if necessary. They outlined which parts of the city were dangerous and instructed citizens to avoid these areas until the chaos subsided.

* * *

Meanwhile, the Giulianis and their allies waited patiently. Luca urged them to avoid the war at all costs; believing sooner or later, it would die down, but it only got worse. The war reached the New York suburbs where the captains and bosses lived. This was a no-no from the accord of the five families. The suburban streets always were filled with children, especially after school. One afternoon, stay-at-home moms and fathers were coming to pick up their children when a driver in a white suit resembling Francesco was leaning on his car, smoking, waiting for Manuel, the younger brother of Francesco. Manuel ran out of the school towards the driver.

"Ciao!" Manuel said getting into the back of the car, throwing his bag on the floor. The driver threw his cigarette and got behind the wheel.

"Ciao, young Manuel," the driver said starting on the car. The merry laughter of the children in the background was covered by a powerful blast resulting in an enormous fire that reached the sky, spitting out black smoke. There was nothing left of the car and its metal parts were scattered all over the once peaceful street. A man, in his sixties, coming to pick up his child was hit by the car door, killing him on the spot. The neighborhood went in chaos. Now, the Saltinottis had gone too far. They didn't consult with the Lombardis or their partners back home before they'd made the hit.

The Giuliani family, devastated, vowed revenge. Sofia cursed every member of the Lombardis, Baldinottis, and Saltinottis for taking her sons away from her. Francesco was long gone and now their youngest son was dead—killed in a war he never took part of.

* * *

The next few days were silent as the families came to a temporary truce. The Italian residents in the city all dressed in black. Everyone came to the funeral except for the Saltinottis. No remains were retrieved so there was only an open-casket. The news media tried attending but were forced to observe a far distance away. During the funeral, Luca sat a few feet away from Michael, holding Sofia's hands. She constantly sobbed and Michael couldn't hold his tears watching the Giulianis endure this pain. Yet, his daughter, Jessica was still missing. After the end of the procession, Luca approached Michael. His eyes were watery but didn't shed a tear. Luca grabbed Michael by the elbow and whispered to his ear,

"Things have gone too far. You can destroy my businesses and the city, but this has gone too far. I have my men searching night and day for your daughter and my son and you do this? You thought this was war? The war starts now, Michael." Luca walked away leaving Michael to ponder what to do next.

When the truce expired, the storm was quickly on its way. Luca, for the first time in a long time, showed every family in New York why the Giulianis were the head Italian family; starting with a spree of surprise raids even in the middle of the day in downtown Manhattan. Every

Saltinotti or Lombardi sympathizer who didn't side with the Giuilianis were executed, extorted, or fled. The pubs and clubs owned by the Lombardis were burnt to the ground and the Giulianis weren't stopping there. Every score by the Lombardis resulted in an even greater one by the Giulianis. They evened the playing field despite losing so much in the beginning. Luca was once again, the most feared boss in the city of New York.

* * *

It's been almost three weeks since Luca's purge and Michael was alone in his office with the lights out, leaning back in his chair. Only his cigarette offered a glimpse of light. He was fighting a war he couldn't possibly win— and mentally accepting the might of Luca. The last words of his rival stuck, like a ball and chain, suffocating him. The Don took a drag, contemplating Luca's next move. He took another when his office door had opened.

Serena entered turning on the lights. "You idiota!" she yelled. "What the hell are you doing?" She said taking a seat.

"Mamma, leave me alone, please."

"Show some respect, you stubborn fool."

"What is it.?"

"Who are you leading out there, a group of toy soldiers?"

"These criminals kidnapped your nipotina."

"I left for a few weeks and I return back to a dumpster fire. Maria Vergine!"

"Mamma, calm down."

"Put out that disgusting thing. It stinks." Serena snatched the cigarette from Luca and smashed it in the ashtray.

" I'm trying to think."

"Your daughter, Michael, is alive and well."

"H—how do you know this? Where is she?"

"I will tell you. But if you do something stupid, Dio help you."

" Tell me! Where is my Jessica?"

"She's in Maine with that kid, Francesco."

"What? He kidnapped her there?"

"No, she left with him!"

"Why would she do such a thing?"

"Because she's in love! Now that she's left. Look what you have done. You start a war with Luca."

"I thought she—"

"You always think you're right. Shut up, Michael."

"Mamma!"

"No, Mamma. Go make peace with Luca and go see your daughter."

"But?"

"But, nothing. Son, your daughter is pregnant and will marry Francesco next week."

"What are you saying.? You must have gone mad!"

"I'm crazy over my nipotina, not you. Here's Jessica's

number. Call her, but first go make peace with Luca. Call off the war."

Michael got up and hugged his mother as tears were running down his cheeks. He sighed from relief but it didn't last long. His Jessica was alive and carrying his first grandchild but the good news didn't diminish the fact that he'd killed Luca's youngest son.

"Thank you, Mamma." he sobbed, like a little boy. "Stop thanking me and go now. Dai!"

""I will. Men, get the car ready!" shouted Michael to his guards, as he hurried out.

* * *

Michael Lombardi and a few of his men were outside the Giuliani Mansion .

"I'm here to speak to Don Luca. My daughter and your son are alive," he yelled loud enough for the guards to hear him. Each man pointed his gun at one another and after a few moments of silence, Luca came out the double iron doors. The Don walked slowly to Michael as each boss signaled to their men to lower their weapons. Michael looked at Luca unimpressed.

"What do you want now?"

"I want to ask for your forgiveness."

"What?"

"I want to admit to my rash behavior!"

"For my son?"

"For everything."

"No apology will ever fix what happened, Michael."

"I know that and I'm sorry."

"Oh, you are. Should I welcome you inside my home?"

"I didn't kill your son. The Saltinottis did so, despite my personal orders not to hurt anyone close to you."

"Why should I care, Michael? I don't care who gave the order. I lost my boy! Both for all I know."

"No! Francesco's alive."

"What are you saying? Where is my son?"

"He's in Maine with my daughter."

"Dead or alive?

"Alive and blessed?"

"How?"

"They're getting married next week. My Jessica is pregnant. You'll be a grandfather, Luca and so will I. Please, won't you forgive me?"

"If this is another trick to win the war Michael, I swear to God, I will burn the whole city to the ground."

"No, no, this is no trick. Serena told me minutes ago. She just got back from Italy."

Tears ran down Michael's face while Luca's heart was feeling heavier just by looking at his broken rival. Luca's eyes watered, too as both men walked further into the courtyard.

"I forgive you Michael but under one condition."

"Anything."

"Each Saltinotti involved in my son's death will die, today."

"They're already dead, Luca. They're resting at the bottom of the sea."

"You really will do this?"

"Luca, I'm no monster but family doesn't cross one another. I just want my daughter back."

"You have her now, I'll have my son and we'll both have our grandchild."

"Si, they are alive and well. I'm told they're in love, Luca."

"We should head to the wedding then?"

"I'm sorry for your loss, Luca."

"I forgive you now, Michael. You've always been a respectful man."

"Thank you."

"No need to thank me. Go home and get ready. We have a wedding to get to."

The war of New York was officially over and New York went peaceful once again. In town, there were remnants of a battlefield, but as fast as the war began, everything was restored to normalcy. The Lombardis and Giuilianis paid for the damages caused to the businesses and helped repair parts of the city.

No-interest loans were given to shop owners including the Chinese. Finally, even for only a few days, there were no extortions or violence. They were the most peaceful days since the end of the Cold War.

24

THE WEDDING

The Lombardi and Giuliani Family

The first lights of the dawn started piercing the night sky as the birds started chirping. It was cold and the smell of dew freshened the scene. The first cars were roaming the town as those who started work early were heading out, the first glimpses of daylight peeking through

Michael Lombardi was parked outside the Giuliani Mansion , leaning on his black Chevrolet, waiting for Luca. A few of his men were nearby in cars waiting for their Don. Luca came out minutes later and embraced Michael, clapping him on the back.

"Everything in place?" The Don asked, looking down at the pavement.

"Yes. Our reinforcements will be here any minute." Michael ordered his men to get ready while he privately talked to Luca. Michael grabbed Luca by the elbow as they walked.

"This is special."

"I agree. I couldn't be happier."

"Me, too, Luca. Shall we hurry then?"

A huge parade of black cars began coming in from the streets and Michael's entourage started up their vehicles. They began the long seven-hour trip from the Giuliani Mansion to Rockport, Maine. Fifty cars crowded I95 North heading down the highway like a trail of black ants carrying food. The Dons vowed to make this the most memorable wedding they have ever attended. Luca's car was the lead which was an honorable gesture for the father of the groom. Luca elected to drive with Sofia by his side. They were silent for nearly the whole trip salvaging what little joy they had left to give their daughter on her best day. Sofia broke the silence, sharing her thoughts.

"Are we going to tell Francesco about his brother?"

"No, Sofia. We can't. Not now."

"He—He has the right to know."

"After the wedding. Maybe weeks after. We'll see"

"Okay. I think that's fair but he will ask about Manuel."

"I know, honey. I'll make up something."

* * *

After the brief conversation, their silence resumed being overheard by the sound of the car engine.

After a few stops for rest, the families finally arrived at Rockport. The small town began filling up with black cars. Men in black suits and tuxedos stopped at every restaurant, diner, and coffee shop with orders to wait for the wedding.

Michael and Luca, along with their relatives headed to the house of Jessica and Francesco. They had a small beach house by the shore, with an excellent view of the ocean. Serena knew the address and within minutes, they spotted the two-story home at the far end of the beach.

* * *

Meanwhile, Jessica had just woken up after a long night of drinking. Both threw each other a bachelor party, making out all over the house in celebration. Jessica planted kisses all over Francesco's face and neck, waking him up.

"Good morning, husband," she said chuckling underneath the sheets.

"No, not yet. I'm still your boyfriend." He went under the sheets kissing her softly as he ran his hand through her hair.

"Do you believe this?"

"No, I don't actually."

"I never thought this day would come for me."

"Me, neither."

"A real family."

"We're almost there."

"So, was this our honeymoon?"

"If it was, we started early. Do you think every day will be like this?"

"I hope so. If I have a say in it, they will be."

"Together."

"Together!"

"I wish our families were here. Don't you?"

"It saddens me my father wouldn't be here to see this."

"One day, we'll actually go back and tell them the big news with a little child. "

"They'll love the child more than they love us."

"They better."

Francesco laughed and hugged Jessica under the sheets. He kissed her again and then got out of bed. As he was heading for the bathroom, the doorbell rang.

"What the fuck? We have neighbors coming around this early?"

"Tell them to go away, sweetheart. I want to spend my day with you only," said Jessica curling up next to Francesco. She could feel his hardness through his boxers, and she moved even closer showing him how wet she was beneath her own underwear. getting naughty. She showed Francesco her vagina and started playing with it, making moaning sounds.

"Yes, ma'am. I will. Stay right there. I mean it—don't move an inch." Francesco came down to the living room with just a pair of black boxers on and opened the door. Expecting a neighbor or Jehovah witnesses to be there, he was surprised to find his father and his mother, there smiling.

"H—how? What are you doing here?" His jaw dropped and couldn't form a complete sentence. His mother hurried to embrace him, squeezing him tightly as his father patted him on the back.

"Good morning, son! I see you're ready for the wedding."

Moments later, Michael and Christina Lombardi entered.

"Hello, Francesco. We hope you're taking good care of our daughter." Michael pretended to act serious, but the joy in his eyes gave him away.

"Of course, Signore Michael. She's upstairs." Francesco's mother was still hugging him. "Ma, let go."

"Why should I let go of my son?"

"Father, please."

"Ok, Sofia. That's enough." As Luca and Sofia sat, Michael and Christina went upstairs, followed by Serena.

"So, you're Francesco. I knew my nipotina would fancy a good-looking man for her husband. Our grand-child will be an angelo." Serena chuckled following behind.

Sofia finally let Francesco loose and started looking at him up and down.

"Francesco, you don't eat well, my boy"

"Mamma, that's the first thing you have to say?"

"I love you son and missed you so much."

"That's better. I missed you too."

"And what's with the mustache?"

"Long story, Mamma."

"May I take a look around?"

"Of course!"

Francesco then turned to his father as his mother went inside the kitchen. "So, Rockport?"

"I missed you too, father."

"You know I missed you, son."

"And I'm sorry for screwing everything up. I didn't want to do more damage."

"It's okay. It doesn't matter now."

"Well—"

"I wish you would have told me where you were heading and about Jessica."

"I was afraid, Dad. Someone tried to kill us."

"But family is family. You know I would have taken care of things."

"I'm sorry. I should have trusted you."

"It's okay, son. I'm glad you're well."

"Where's Manuel? I owe him an apology."

"He is sick, so we couldn't bring him along."

"Don't tell me he didn't want to come to my wedding."

"No. He was coming, but we had to take him to the hospital. He sends his regards. Don't worry."

"Ok, the first thing when I come back will be to take him out for ice cream. Please tell him."

"I will. Don't worry."

Luca then hugged his son, holding back the tears that were prickling behind his eyes. His voice cracked and his voice became heavier.

"Where's the bathroom?"

"First door on the left, Pa." Francesco smiled, believing his father was overwhelmed with joy.

* * *

Meanwhile, Jessica was lying on the bed, naked waiting for Francesco to come back.

She heard footsteps approaching and yelled, "Did you send them away?" Jessica rolled over showing her backside bare.

"No, he couldn't."

Jessica jumped out of the bed and quickly covered herself. She found her father, next to her mother and grandmother behind them.

"Mom? Dad? Grandma! What the hell are you doing here?"

"Surprise!" her father said lifting and spinning her around.

"Dad, I can't breathe" Jessica grumbled as Michael put her down but hugged her still.

"Nonna! Is this your doing?" Jessica said unsure why they had come.

"Yes, nipotina. Look how happy your mother and father are. They couldn't miss your wedding."

Jessica's mother, Christina was crying. "Oh sweetheart, I can't believe you did this to us."

"Mom, it's okay."

"Why you didn't tell me, Jessica? We almost killed everyone in New York" her father said.

"Well, you wouldn't approve of my choices. And we almost got killed, too."

"But—"

"You know you would've forbade me from marrying a Giuliani."

"Hush, Jessica," said her mother.

"Yes, your father's a man of many mistakes," said Michael.

"Finally, the big man admits."

"I'm sorry. That's why I'm here."

"To say you're sorry, father?"

"To ask for your forgiveness. And answer your husband's request for my daughter."

"Dad, why are you acting so different?"

"I am, honey. I've learned a lot while you were away."

"So, do I have your blessing for this wedding…"

"You do."

"And will you love my child more than you love me?"

"I already love the little guy."

"It might be a girl."

"It better be a girl," her grandmother shouted.

Everyone smiled and Jessica told her parents to give her a second to get changed.

Then, she found her parents and everyone else downstairs, surrounded by the smell of espresso.

"My mother insisted on making coffee for everyone!" Francesco shrugged, sitting in the living room next to his father. Jessica went to the Don and kissed him on the cheek.

"So, all of us are here after all."

"They are except for my little brother. He's sick," Francesco said smiling and holding Jessica.

"Thank me, young man!" Serena shouted sitting from across him.

"Grazie, signorina," Francesco said bowing.

"Oh, shut up. Call me nonna from now on. Nonna Serena."

"Ok, Nonna," Francesco expressed awkwardly.

"Is it just you only, Mamma and Papa? Where's Giovanni?"

"Everyone came. Giovanni's with the men and elders." Luca grabbed a mug from the tray Sofia left on the table.

"Where's Federico?" Francesco asked his father.

"Yes, he even came. He's with Giovanni."

"Wow! This is bigger than I expected," Francesco whispered to Jessica, causing her to giggle.

Michael took a sip, with his eyes squinting, making a weird noise as he swallowed.

"You don't drink espresso, Michael? Do you?" Luca joked, taking a sip.

"It's been a while. I forgot how bitter it tastes," he

said, asking Christina to bring him a glass of water. Luca laughed, patting him on the back.

"So, where's the wedding taking place?" Michael asked.

"We were having it on the beach. There's a nice pavilion that is gorgeous where the sun sets."

"How romantic!" said Michael. "

I like it already," said Sophia.

"We should tell the men to prepare the area," Michael said getting up.

"How many?" Francesco asked curiously.

"Everyone!" said Michael and Luca at the same time, cheering.

"We took fifty cars." As Michael was talking, Jessica while sipping her coffee, almost spit it out when she heard the numbers.

"Wait a minute! You took fifty cars and drove all the way here?"

"Yes my dear! We had to bring some things for the wedding." Michael walked to the door and stopped.

"Francesco, I need you for a minute. Come here." The Don grabbed his hat from the coat rack as his son accompanied him.

"What is it, signore?"

"I want some money for the bouquet and don't be cheap." Michael smiled putting out his hand.

"I always hated that custom, father," Francesco laughed giving his father some hundreds."

"And where's that pavilion exactly? I want to place a

few things there—" Michael paused for a moment and then said,

"Oh, I didn't forget about the rest of you. You're coming along, too."

The rest of the family got up sighing but happy to see their beloved children happy in one piece.

* * *

For a few hours, Michael Lombardi led the family members and guards in groups of five to the pavilion area. The place was going to be a gala built on the edge of the cape. The cape was covered in a yellowish withered grass and the trees at its entrance shielded those hired to construct and clean the area. As the afternoon's sun began to set, it headed behind the mountains, offering a stunning sunset.

Michael and Luca wanted something memorable. The families and workers, under Michael's command, began laying out white chairs, on the left and the right of the cape, forming a small aisle in the middle, filled with pots with lilies. Lilies were Jessica's favorite flower. Sofia and Christina spent time with some of their young ones, picking lilies and making a beautiful bouquet. At the end of the cape, a wedding altar was constructed entirely from white wood. The family members also erected an arch, filled with bouquets of lilies. The pavilion was now surrounded by white tulles, as if it was a concert, preventing anyone who was not invited from coming inside.

The guards were there and went over instructions on securing the area.

The wedding was two hours away when Michael returned after taking a nap with Sofia at a nearby hotel.

"Everything looks ready?" he said, holding a big white box.

"Dad, what's that?" asked Jessica.

"Did you buy your wedding dress? I thought you'd like to wear this little turquoise one I bought yesterday."

"No, we weren't having anything big."

"Then wear this, my daughter." Michael opened the box revealing a beautiful dress. It had a modern touch to it, not like the traditional Italian wedding dresses. Jessica hugged her father, grateful for his kind gesture.

"Thank you, Papa."

"Nipotina, the esposa must see herself in the mirror," her grandmother said. "I'll help you with the dress." Serena made her way upstairs. "Come, come, don't waste time." She signaled to Jessica who was still hugging her father.

"Ok, Nonna." She grabbed the box and followed her grandmother. Michael then went to Francesco.

"I brought you your toc ferro as well."

"I thought you weren't into that tradition."

"Just put it in your pocket, Francesco," the Don said giving him the piece of iron he thoughts the groom should have in his pocket during the wedding.

"Thank you, signore," Francesco said bowing.

* * *

The sun was now setting, covering the city of Rockport with its beautiful orange glow. Jessica, now dressed in her wedding gown was walking barefoot on the beach. Everything was calm, except for the sound of the waves, which leaped for Jessica's feet. Michael and Christina were by her side, walking their daughter to the cape. This was the proudest moment in their lives. Their daughter was getting married and carrying their grandchild. After all the hardships, the families finally made it together. Their children would spend the rest of their lives happily ever after.

Francesco was already waiting in the cape, under the arch, holding a bouquet of lilies. Seated, was a sea of men and women dressed in tuxedos and summer dresses. Federico was by his side as his best man. Luca was entrusted to be the one to perform the ceremony, binding Francesco and Jessica forever in eternal love, into one happy family. Everyone sat, waiting patiently for Jessica to appear.

"Can you believe this?" Federico whispered to Francesco.

"I really don't."

"You made it."

"Really? A good friend."

"I told you I'd be a zio."

"I should have listened to you."

"You made it."

"We made it."

"How's the pub?"

"That's a story for another time."

"You can open a pub here."

"You think?"

"We need a good Italian pub here. I'm tired of the shitty Irish beers."

"Something to think about."

"The wine here is shit and don't even get me started the shitty pizza."

"What about the gin?"

"The gin's good according to Jess."

"Then, I'll come to teach them a few tricks."

"You can get a house across the beach."

"Oh, I don't want to see your face *every* day, my friend."

"We could barbecue every Sunday."

"That's tempting."

Francesco hugged Federico— a hug that a brother gives to another— a hug that meant more than anything ever said.

"Grazie," Federico whispered with tears flowing.

"Stop it you, you're making me look soft."

Federico laughed patting Francesco on the back.

The suspense was saturating the attendees and Luca told the guests to be patient. Michael had paid for a band, which was waiting for the bride to appear through the trees before they would start playing.

The ceremony was grander than anyone's wildest dreams. This was the biggest moment of the young couple's lives and the crowd hushed as Jessica finally arrived. The air was filled with harmony with the traditional wedding song, Chen a Luna. Jessica walked to the altar smiling—a smile no one had ever seen on her face. Her eyes met Francesco's and he couldn't stop looking at her. She saw Giovanni, sitting in the first row, right before the arch. Jessica smiled and her brother bowed. Michael walked Jessica to the wedding arch.

"Take care of her," Michael said both as an order and a threat to Francesco who merely smiled in return.

"I will, signore."

"Call me, Papa." Michael winked and took a seat on the first row.

"Ok, Big papa." Francesco chuckled turning to Jessica.

"You're breathtaking."

"I love you."

"I love you, too."

"Can you believe it?"

"It's so cool."

"Our families are together."

"Yes, they are! This was the greatest gift of all."

"Now, we'll be together forever."

"Together, with no worries. Always?"

"Always, Jessica my love."

"I love you so much."

"I love you so much!"

Luca waited as they finished their conversation as the couple turned towards him for the ceremony to begin.

* * *

Luca cleared his throat.

"Buonasera, amici e famiglia. Our children today are getting married. Despite our family differences, despite our stupid feud, the ages of battles about territories, and our stupid businesses, our children decided to shape a new path for our families going forward." Luca paused taking a deep breath. His chest felt heavy and his heart was racing as tears ran down his face.

"A new path for all of us—a path of peace, a path of repentance, and a path of true Italian heritage. I want to thank my son and my new daughter for their gift. This is the most beautiful present a person can receive—family, love, and peace. Francesco and Jessica, I thank you both from the depths of my heart and I want to apologize here, in front of everyone, for not being by your sides from the very beginning. Thank you!" Luca pressed his eyes with his fingers, trying to contain his emotions. . He wiped more tears away and opened a small leather Bible.

"Time for the service," Luca said loudly and everyone in the audience cheered.

The guests' cheer was interrupted by police sirens growing in volume as sound of tires screeching neared the pavilion. One gunshot broke up the bliss. Everybody stood still, fixed into their positions, turning their heads towards the trees at the bottom of the cape. The sun was quickly setting, shrouding everything in darkness which was pierced by dozens of flashlights, spotlighted on the wedding.

25

SACRIFICING EVERYTHING

The FBI

The morning the war had started between the families of New York, Thomas was in his office, in front of the board with all the evidence he collected. The place had a claustrophobic feeling. Anyone who came inside, saw the files piling up, nearly ready to fall down. Thomas, with a cigarette in his mouth, was trying to connect the dots; trying to find at something to put on either one of the families. Someone knocked, pulling him out of his thoughts.

"Come in." Garcia entered with a worried look on her face.

"Sir, there was a shooting in Castello di Vino."

"What? Calm down, Garcia."

"Sir, someone had ripped Castello di Vino apart."

"Do we have any suspects?"

"No, a bystander called 911 from a payphone."

"Are there officers on the scene?"

"The 3rd Precinct got there first, sir. They're already interrogating the witness."

"Tell them to stand by until I get there."

Thomas grabbed his coat and drove down to Castello di Vino, which looked like a war zone. He passed under the yellow tape, crunching on the shattered glasses. The rain washed away possible evidence, but he knew it was a mob hit. Agent Miller showed his badge to the officers and stepped inside. He found a barman, standing behind the counter, talking with a police officer. "Officer, I'll take it from here. Thank you." The officer sighed as he left.

"Good morning, sir. I believe you remember me."

"Ciao. Oh, I do. You were here the other day to talk to a customer."

"Yes. Francesco Giuliani. Do you know him?"

"Oh, I never got his name."

"Lying is not going to help you Mr.—?"

"Federico Rosso."

"Mr. Rosso, have you seen Francesco?"

"That man may have come by once in the last week."

"Anything time else?"

"No, sir. I believe that man is a model citizen. We only have good people as customers come inside here."

"Did you see the shooters."

"No sir, I did not."

"Were you drinking, Federico?"

"I might have been. It's not against the law."

"No, it's not. Were you drinking alone?"

"I like doing that from time to time; gets me ready for work."

"Why then are there three glasses here in front of you?"

"They must have fallen off the counter."

"Ok, cut the bullshit and tell me where's Francesco."

"I told you, I don't know the man."

"I'll find him. He's in deep shit."

"Oh, they're long gone—"

"What was that?"

"Nothing, sir. I believe he won't come here for some time until I fix this place up. That's what I was saying."

"Come by my precinct to give a statement today. You'll love the place."

"Addio, investigatore."

Thomas came outside and Garcia was waiting, holding a black umbrella. Thomas got under it and lit a cigarette. He took a long drag and Garcia tried waving the smoke away. "So, did we find anything, sir?"

"No. It's just—"

"Just what sir?"

"He said they're long gone."

"What did he mean?"

"That's what he said. They're long gone."

"Who?"

"He told me that when I warned him about Francesco."

"They're long gone? Sounds like Francesco and another person?"

"Yes, it does."

"Is he coming to give a statement?"

"I don't know. He's not cooperating and I have nothing to hold him on. But let's assume he's referring to Francesco, I bet whoever is with him is someone of importance. Let's get back to the station. I need to look over my notes."

* * *

They drove back and spent days trying to figure out what was behind Federico's words. Thomas made a list of all suspected associates that Francesco was known to hang out with, ranging from Fredrico, to Luca to his little brother.

After a few days of rigorous investigating, Agent Garcia ran inside Thomas' office. Her hair was a mess and she looked tired. She tried talking but she needed a moment to catch her breath. "Garcia, is everything alright?"

"No, sir."

"What's wrong."

"I received over ten phone calls today, sir. The city is at war."

"I mean we already know that, Garcia!"

"No, there is a real war on the streets for control. The mob families are at war."

"So, you're saying they have declared war amongst themselves?"

"Yes, sir. Castello was only the beginning."

"Why? It doesn't make sense. They were working together."

"I'm not sure yet, sir but precincts are reporting an increased number of arsons and killings that are mob-related around the city."

"Well, get on."

"Sir, Quantico demanded you do something, right?"

"Yeah, yeah but I don't want just the petty gangsters."

"So, we're not going to do something?"

"No, we're not. We'll wait."

"But why, sir?"

"If the families are at war, the precincts and their corrupt cops will be at war as well. Then, it'll be just you and me, investigating contaminated crime scenes. We'll apprehend a few thugs at best, which do us no good. We want the big fish; Luca, Michael, Francesco, and Giovanni. Let these petty mobsters kill one other until we're ready. Less work for us."

"O—okay sir. I'll inform my team to stand down."

Thomas ignored the arrest reports that came in almost hourly. The 5th precinct, much like the streets of New York was in disorder. Criminals were brought in almost every minute and being released within hours if they didn't have mob ties. Detectives were getting warrants for the Italian businesses across the city but the leads were spotty. Garcia came to the office the next morning with a folder in her hand.

"Good morning, Sir. I found something."

"What do you have there?"

"Rumor has it, that Jessica Lombardi has been kidnapped."

"Another lie that doesn't make sense."

"I know sir. It's farfetched but it's a lead."

"Now, tour informance have reached an all-time low."

"My thoughts, exactly."

Thomas opened the file and found nothing of importance except for some credit card payments. "Why was she staying at the Hotel Plaza more than three times in a week?" Thomas wondered.

"Who knows? Maybe she had a boyfriend she was hiding," Garcia said shyly.

"Wait a minute. That's it."

"What is it, sir?"

"They're long gone."

"The pub owner's phrase again?"

"Yes. What if Mr. Rocco was referring to Francesco and Jessica?"

Thomas and Garcia sat for hours trying to figure out if there was a connection but two rival family members in love was a long shot. They got warrants on the banks to give up any bank statements on Jessica and Francesco.

They traced there were times Francesco stayed in the Plaza Hotel and used his credit card with his own name on it.

"Francesco, my friend, you're getting sloppy." said Agent Miller after hanging up with the bank.

The war got worse when they got the call that Manuel Giuliani, the son of Michael, was killed by an IED outside his school. Yet, they continued biding their time. Thomas and Garcia along with a few other agents watched all the videotapes of Plaza Hotel, showing Jessica and Francesco staying there, over ten times in the past month alone.

"Garcia, this is it. Jessica is with Francesco."

"But where?"

"That's the mystery."

"They probably are using cash. The airports had already known to alert authorities if Francesco or any mafia member left New York. So, they either left by bus, train or ship?"

"What if they left the country?"

"Then, we're fucked. Let's hope not. Let the war play out and keep a close eye on the captains. Ask our captain for more resources. Maybe he'll give a fuck now that he's under more pressure than ever to produce results."

* * *

The 'Bloodshed' articles reached Thomas' office who was locked inside for days, trying to figure out the families' next move with the two rival siblings missing. Luca and Michael were smarter—they remained out of the spotlight and so did Thomas. He waited patiently, letting the city bleed until he could cut the heads off once and for all. There would be no compromises and there would be no deals.

Thomas kept hunting but he couldn't find a single lead tying the family heads to any of these cases.

* * *

Oddly, the city lived once again in silence. The trail of clues started going cold and Agent Miller was desperate for results. He needed the war to go on for just one mistake.

Agent Garcia found Agent Miller sleeping inside his office when she barged in. She threw some pictures on Thomas' desk, waking him.

"The families had a meeting with Luca and Michael."

"When?"

"Yesterday evening."

"And?"

"This is the reason why all is silent."

"If there's a truce, they must have found the two lovebirds."

"But we don't know just yet."

"A war ends because of two kids? What a fairytale!"

"Could be. Maybe they were killed."

"If they were, this city would burn to the ground. However, Garcia, I think this is a long shot. I believe Jessica and Francesco ran away from their parents because they are hiding their love."

"Ok, but to where?"

"Who knows, they're in love? Maybe Great Adventure?"

"Stop joking around, Agent Miller."

"Okay, okay. Let's beef up our officers near the Mansions. If I'm correct, they'll lead us right to Jessica and Francesco. If they don't, my career is over."

"Sir—"

"I know, Garcia. This is a gamble that I'm willing to take. I didn't join the force to catch petty gangsters. I'm willing to take the heat on this one."

"Ok, I'm on it, sir."

Garcia left, leaving Thomas doubting his instincts for the first time in his career. It was a gamble he was willing to bet his career on. For some odd reason, although farfetched, this motive made perfect sense to him. All he needed to make the biggest arrest in his career was to find just one of them packing a weapon that could be traced back to the Bloodshed. For now, all Agent Thomas Miller has to do was wait for the right moment to strike hard.

26

BLEEDING OUT

The Giuliani Family, The Lombardi Family, and the FBI

For Thomas, it was the longest week of his entire career. Every day the city was silent, it was another blow for Thomas who started to believe he was chasing a dead lead. He began feeling guilty for the innocent lives taken during the mob war, often complaining when Garcia came by. They smoked in silence. Thomas' chest was hurting while Garcia was sitting still. There were no new leads and the duo felt like they were officially out of work.

"Maybe we should accept that our careers are finally coming to an end, Garcia."

"Sir, I still believe in you."

"It's been a week and nothing."

"I know."

"I sent out a fucking APB to every precinct from Wisconsin to Texas and still nothing."

"By the way, the Quantico called earlier. They want us to fly down there first thing tomorrow morning and give them an update, sir."

"I guess big brother is calling us home. It's over."

"It was a pleasure working with you, sir."

"Garcia, you proved a lot more useful than I imagined."

"Thank you, sir?" It came out more like a question.

"I hope your career doesn't end like mine. Tell them you were against my orders."

"No, sir. I am with you until the end. I will back you."

"Garcia, don't let an old man like me destroy the rest of your young career."

"It'll be an honor to go down with you, sir."

"Were you always this stubborn?"

"Always, sir."

Thomas lit a cigarette as his second-in-command had him smiling. Garcia was giggling. It was a sigh of relief despite being devastated by their failure to apprehend the crime bosses. Thomas took a bottle of whiskey out from the drawer. "One last drink for mankind?"

"Yes, sir, I'll take one today."

Thomas poured two glasses and as he did so, his phone rang.

"Hello?" He answered with an exhausted expression that quickly turned attentive.

"Where?" Miller's right hand was trembling, and Garcia grew concerned.

"Call the FBI there and tell them to get ready." He slammed the phone down.

"We found them!" Miller said, going for his coat.

"Where?" Garcia stood up excited.

"Rockport, Maine."

"How?"

"Fifty black cars just went through the toll booths minutes ago. They have snapshots of Luca driving one of them."

"Sir, we don't have arrest warrants. We have nothing on them."

"Fuck the warrants. Let me handle this. We'll have them by the time we arrived."

"I'll call the Bureau for back up."

"Get us two tickets to Maine. Let's go!"

* * *

The captain was told to remain behind as a special police escort took Agent Garcia and Miller to the airport. Garcia was excited, not only because this was the first big takedown of her career, but she was finally glad to put a stop to the mob families' presence in New York City. She couldn't remain still, tapping her leg on the floor, eager to get to Rockport.

Thomas was relaxing serious, but the Agent didn't have a plan on what he would arrest the family heads' on.

He didn't have enough evidence for a slam dunk case, but he couldn't let them escape, not today. Not on the day, the most notorious New York mobsters would be all gathered in a single spot. Agent Miller was willing to sacrifice everything including his career to take them down once and for all.

The agents boarded the plane and 50 minutes later they arrived at Rockport Airport. A bureau car; a black Chrysler with black tinted windows was waiting for them. They got in and headed to a local precinct where the bureau's backup was already there with debriefing preparations.

* * *

Two hours before the wedding, Thomas Miller and Agent Garcia were in the control room with officers from the Rockport Police Department and FBI agents. He lit a cigarette and took a seat at the edge of the desk; all eyes in the room were on him. He took a drag and cleared his throat.

"For those who don't know me, my name is Special Agent Thomas Miller. I've been an FBI agent for the past twenty years. My first case revolved around cases involving the Scarfo and Bruno crime families in Philadelphia. We had a strong feeling back then that their activities were in sync with the New York crime families which ultimately proved to be so. I have dedicated my career to destroy organized crime and today I get the chance to put an end to it in New York once and for all." Thomas paused taking another drag. His hands were sweating.

"I will not accept failure today. I will not accept anyone fucking this up. I trust each one of you will do as told. This is a case that will advance your careers. These are arrests that only a few people can brag about having on their records. So, listen closely. We're there to arrest them. Do not bother yourselves with legal responsibilities, I'll make sure everything goes down smoothly. Are we clear here?"

Thomas put out his cigarette and the officers yelled. "Yes, sir!"

"Get your guns, gear, and get ready," Thomas said already exiting the room with Garcia.

Everyone got into their service cars, with Thomas and Garcia's car leading the way. They advanced towards the cape, where the wedding was just about to begin. An informant who was constructing the wedding site gave them the exact location. The sirens were on, echoing throughout the silent townships, casting blue, red and white lights in the dusky streets. When the police cars approached the cape, the loud cheers heard from a distance quickly stopped.

Thomas got out of his car first, running between the trees, to scope out the wedding scene. The agents got out almost after him but lost track of the agent who was already yards away. Garcia saw Thomas run into the woods nearby and was unable to call him out. Thomas saw a few sentries leaning on the pines. He took out his service weapon; a Glock 17 and shot the first one he saw. The gun blast echoed through the cape as a henchman fell yelling with a bullet wound in his chest. Thomas shot, again and again, killing two more henchmen.

The officers ran after Thomas but froze, not knowing what was going on. Moments later, Agent Garcia and officers started running towards the cape as yelling could be heard from the other side.

Thomas kept moving until he reached an area filled with purple ribbons. He stood on the flower petals that had fallen to the ground. The men stood up, surprised. They started reaching for their guns. It's been a while since Thomas had used his service weapon, but his gun skills kicked in. He aimed at Luca and shot at him three times; twice in the chest and one that missed. Thomas kept firing; taking cover. The family members had shot back as Don Luca was falling, hitting the ground. He was dead before his head bashed on the wooden platform, under the arch, causing the bible to fall off, on his Francesco's foot. His son's foot was soaked in a pool of his own blood, as the bullet that missed Luca hit Francesco in the stomach. The FBI and the agents raced ahead shooting more family members who pulled guns on them. Serena took a bullet wound to the shoulder, causing her to fall to the ground. She screamed in pain; slowly dying. Her face was submerged in the beach's sand.

Giovanni and the rest of the male family members

started firing back towards the direction of the FBI agents. A barrage of bullets flew in every direction. The heavy rains of New York found a new port; a rain of shells, blood, and death. The officers took cover in the pines returned the fire. The women and children ran by them, causing chaos, like an angry sea. Some were struck escaping and most were apprehended once they exited the forest.

Giovanni, Michael, and a few henchmen had Agent Miller surrounded and shot at him consecutively; striking him. His body was lying in the middle of the anarchy; women and children ran by stepping on him. His body had countless bullet wounds and he was still alive; choking on his blood as someone crushed his ribs, stepping over him to find refuge. Giovanni walked up to him and shot as

Jessica screamed when she saw Francesco in a pool of blood.

"No! No! Don't you dare leave me!" She ran over to him and collapsed in a violent sob on his chest.

Michael got hit running to save Jessica but was still alive.

The gunshots and screaming were chaotic, but Jessica pay it no mind. The death of Francesco who was going to be her husband was a devastating blow. Jessica wailed over her husband-to-be's body.

* * *

The agents moved in and within minutes, had secured the area. The place which was a wedding scene now became a battlefield— a scene only reminiscent in war documentaries. Bodies were lying everywhere across the cape while rivers of blood flowed out to the sea. Most of the surviving males of both families surrendered, including Giovanni. They dropped their weapons and put their hands above their heads. Hundreds of officers were on the scene putting them in handcuffs and pointing their guns. Garcia looked around everywhere for Thomas Miller, but couldn't find him.

She saw Jessica, still wailing, in her wedding dress, under the arch. She rushed onstage to get Jessica.

"Signorina, please," Garcia said softly. Jessica was shaking; her ears only heard constant buzzing.

"Signorina, are you hit?" Garcia felt sorry not knowing what her first-in-command was plotting beforehand.

"Murderers!" Jessica screamed over and over. "You took my baby away. My love! You killed my family. Murderers! I curse you forever!"

The police put the family members in the squad cars one by one, starting with Federico and Giovanni. Jessica was still lying on Francesco's cold body.

"My baby—My family," she sobbed. Agent Garcia put handcuffs on her and gently hauled her up. Jessica didn't know her grandmother, mother, and father-in-law, Luca were killed. Her father was rushed to the hospital in critical condition. All she cared about was that the man she loved—the father of her child was shot dead.

" I want Francesco back." she kept saying as she was escorted to Garcia's service car.

When she closed the back door, she noticed a letter, folded on Thomas' seat. She put it in her pocket.

"I will kill you all. I will curse you forever for what you have done," yelled Jessica from the back seat.

"Agent Garcia, should we cuff her legs?" an officer asked.

Once Jessica was secured inside the SWAT car, Garcia stepped away to read Thomas' letter.

To Garcia, my best partner in crime,

You now think I'm irrational and crazy. That I'm a stupid old man who made a bad choice. I assure you, everything you think of me is true. I spent most of my life hunting down mobsters, I also spent my life getting stomped by the bad laws of our country. Somehow, my life was only dedicated to hunting monsters that I couldn't catch.

Today was the day, I finally caught them. There was no way we could charge them; they were too smart. Someone had to take one for the team and that someone was me. Don't follow my footsteps. Carve your own way to success, Garcia.

Today, the FBI and citizens finally won the battle

against organized crime. You never knew this, but now I finally have peace with my wife who was caught in the crossfire of a family war, killed by Luca Giuliani's men years ago. I can finally rest. Thank you for being on my side.

Partner up, Garcia.

* * *

These were Thomas Miller's final words—the last he left in this world. That and a huge mess, ruining the lives of the crime families, the same way they ruined his.

She went to the car and looked at Jessica, who was starring solemnly through the gated window in front of her.

"Signorina, you'll be out soon if we have nothing on you. I'm sorry for your loss."

Garcia started the car and drove her to the nearest police department where she would be interrogated until proven innocent.

The silence at the cape resumed, marking its place as the Bloodshed. The seagulls weren't chirping, and the waves were deadened. The blood of the victims at the cape kept flowing into the sea, gradually disappearing into the ocean. This was the end of the New York families and the agent who sacrificed everything to take them down.